# DOCTOR WHO
### AND THE
# WEB OF FEAR

*Also available from BBC Books:*

# DOCTOR WHO
## AND THE
# WEB OF FEAR

Based on the BBC Television serial *The Web of Fear* by Mervyn Haisman and Henry Lincoln by arrangement with the BBC

## TERRANCE DICKS

BOOKS

1 3 5 7 9 10 8 6 4 2

BBC Books, an imprint of Ebury Publishing
20 Vauxhall Bridge Road,
London SW1V 2SA

BBC Books is part of the Penguin Random House group of companies
whose addresses can be found at global.penguinrandomhouse.com

Penguin
Random House
UK

Published by BBC Books in 2016
First published in 1976 by Universal-Tandem Publishing Co. Ltd.

www.eburypublishing.co.uk

A CIP catalogue record for this book is available from the British Library

ISBN 978 1 785 94036 1

Editorial Director: Albert DePetrillo
Editorial Manager: Grace Paul
Series Consultant: Justin Richards
Cover design: Lee Binding © Woodlands Books Ltd, 2016
Cover illustration: Chris Achilleos
Production: Alex Goddard

Typeset in India by Thomson Digital Pvt Ltd, Noida, Delhi

Printed and bound in the USA

# Contents

# The Changing Face of Doctor Who

## The Second Doctor

This *Doctor Who* novel features the second incarnation of the Doctor. After his first encounter with the Cybermen, the Doctor changed form. His old body was apparently worn out, and so he replaced it with a new, younger one. The scratchy, arrogant old man that had been the First Doctor was replaced with a younger and apparently far softer character. The First Doctor's cold, analytical abilities give way to apparent bluster and a tendency to panic under pressure.

But with the Second Doctor more than any other, first impressions are misleading. The Doctor's apparent bluster and ineptitude masks a deeper, darker nature. But there are moments too when the Second Doctor's humanity also shines through. There is ultimately no doubt that his raison d'etre is to fight the evil in the universe.

## Jamie

James Robert Macrimmon is the son of Donald Macrimmon, and a piper like his father and his father's father. Coming from 1746, Jamie is simple and straightforward, but he is also intelligent and blessed with a good deal of common sense. Almost everything is new to him, and while he struggles to understand he also enjoys the experience. Jamie is also extremely brave, never one to shirk a fight or run away.

Ultimately, Jamie sees the Doctor as a friend as well as a mentor. While he relishes the chance to travel and learn and have adventures, he also believes that the Doctor really does need his help.

### Victoria

Victoria is a reluctant adventurer. She travels with the Doctor through necessity rather than choice after her father was exterminated by the Daleks, leaving her stranded on Skaro. Until she was kidnapped by the Daleks, Victoria led a sheltered and unsophisticated life. But she is clever and intelligent.

Despite the fact that both tease her at every opportunity, Victoria cares deeply for the Doctor and Jamie. But while she enjoys her time in their company, she still misses her father. She remains forever an unwilling adventurer.

# 1

## Return of Evil

The huge, furry monster reared up, as if to strike. Well over seven feet tall, its immensely broad body made it seem squat and lumpy. It had the huge hands of a gorilla, the savage yellow fangs and fierce red eyes of a grizzly bear.

There was no fear in the face of the white-bearded old man who stood looking up at it, just a yearning curiosity. He knew the monster wouldn't move. It had stood like this, in the private museum, for over forty years, ever since he had brought it back from Tibet. He reached up and opened a flap in the monster's chest. Beneath was an empty space, just large enough to hold a small sphere.

The door opened and two people walked in. One was a tall, elegant white-haired old man, the other an attractive young girl. The man pointed to the brooding figure at the end of the hall. 'There he is, Miss Travers. Now, please, you take him away!' Although his voice was cultured, it held traces of a middle-European accent.

Anne Travers was used to apologising for the eccentricities of her father. 'I'll do my best, Mr Julius.' She smiled and crossed over to her father. 'Hello, Father.'

Professor Travers looked round in mild surprise. 'Hello, Anne. Thought you were in America.'

Anne Travers sighed. 'I *was* in America—until you cabled saying you were in trouble. You were supposed to meet me at the airport.'

'I was? Thought I'd better come here and have another go at Julius—the silly old fool won't listen to me.'

The museum owner marched angrily over to them. 'Me, a fool? You would like me to be a fool, Professor Travers—fool enough to give you back my Yeti!'

'You *must* give it back, at least for a time. Don't you understand, the thing is dangerous.'

Julius flung out one hand in a dramatic gesture. 'Forty years it stands in my museum! Now he tells me it is dangerous, but Julius is not so easily tricked.'

The two old men glared angrily at each other. Travers shabby and unkempt with tangled hair and bushy beard, Julius tall and elegant in his beautifully cut suit. Anne sighed again. She glanced at the placard at the feet of the rearing monster. It read, 'Life-size model of the Yeti, commonly known as the Abominable Snowman. Brought back from Tibet by Mr Edward Travers after his expedition of 1935.'

2

It had all happened long before Anne Travers was born. Edward Travers, with his friend and colleague Angus Mackay, had gone in search of the Abominable Snowman, the legendary man—beast rumoured to haunt the snowy passes of Tibet. Months later Travers had returned, alone. Mackay had been killed on the expedition. Travers had told a wild story of *faked* Abominable Snowmen, robot servants of some alien Intelligence that planned to take over the world. The plot had been foiled by a mysterious being known only as 'the Doctor'. Travers had brought back a strange collection of objects in support of his story. They included the massive creature that now stood in the museum, and a small silver sphere that, he claimed, had once controlled the creature and given it life.

Travers had been unable to prove his claims. The sphere remained silent, the Yeti refused to stir, and everyone assumed Travers, unbalanced by his sufferings in Tibet, was attempting an elaborate fraud.

Although no one believed the story, it had created a considerable stir. As a result, Emil Julius, a wealthy and eccentric collector with his own private museum, had offered to buy the Yeti for a handsome sum. Dejected, discredited, almost penniless, Travers accepted the offer—an action he was to regret for the rest of his life.

Although he sold the Yeti itself, Travers kept the silver sphere which controlled it, together with a number of other Yeti relics. Determined to justify

3

himself to the world, he had begun to examine the sphere with the aim of discovering its secrets. With incredible determination he had embarked upon the study of the still-new science of electronics. In forty years Travers had turned himself from a discredited anthropologist into a world-famous scientist. His discoveries and inventions had made him rich and respected. But all this time he never lost sight of his one central aim, to reanimate the control sphere and bring the Yeti back to life. Anne, now a scientist herself, had grown up with stories of her father's adventures in Tibet. The strange Doctor and his two companions were like figures in a fairy-tale to her. She knew Travers had made repeated attempts to buy back the Yeti, but Emil Julius was as obstinate as Travers himself. The more determined Travers became to get the Yeti back, the more determined was Julius to keep it, convinced he was the owner of something valuable and unique. Looking at the two angry old men, Anne saw their quarrel had lost none of its bitterness, though both were now into their seventies.

Taking her father to one side she said quietly, 'You know Mr Julius won't sell the Yeti back. Why all this urgency?'

Travers lowered his voice. 'I've *done* it, Anne. At last I've reactivated the control sphere. It began signalling again!'

'That's wonderful news, Father,' said Anne soothingly.

'It would be—except for one thing. The control sphere's disappeared.' He turned angrily back towards Julius. 'Don't you see, it will try to return to the Yeti—and if I'm not there when it does... Oh, make him understand, Anne.'

Julius interrupted, 'I understand well enough. You try to scare me, to get your Yeti back. Well, it is priceless, the only one in the world, and it is mine!'

Anne took her father's arm. 'We'd better go. Maybe you put the sphere away somewhere and forgot where—it's happened before.'

'I tell you I've looked...'

'Then we'll go back and look again. You know I can always find things for you.' Gently she led him away.

Julius escorted them to the front door, closed it behind them. He stood for a moment, shaking with rage. 'No one destroys Emil Julius's collection—no one.' Still grumbling childishly to himself he began to lock and bar the door.

In the empty hall, the Yeti stood motionless, surrounded by devil-masks, mummies, dinosaur bones and all the other oddities of Julius's collection. Then a faint signal, a kind of electronic bleeping, disturbed the silence. It seemed to come from outside the window. Suddenly the glass shattered, broken by the impact of a silver sphere. It was as if the sphere had been hurled through the window from the street outside. But the silver missile did not drop to the ground. It hovered in mid-air. Then it floated slowly towards the Yeti and disappeared into the still open hollow in the creature's chest. Immediately the flap closed over it.

Alarmed by the noise of smashing glass, Julius ran into the room. He stopped, seeing the shattered window, the glass on the floor. Was the old fool Travers so insane he was now throwing bricks through the window? Julius looked out. The street below was silent and deserted.

Julius decided to telephone the police. On his way out of the hall, he stopped for another look at his beloved Yeti. He gazed proudly up at it. The Yeti's eyes opened and glared redly into his own.

Appalled Julius took a pace back. The Yeti stepped off its stand, following him. Its features blurred and shimmered before his horrified eyes, becoming even more fierce and wild than before. With a sudden, shattering roar the Yeti smashed down its arm in a savage blow...

The mysterious and brutal murder of Emil Julius, together with the disappearance of the pride of his collection, caused a tremendous sensation. Because of their past association, Professor Travers came briefly under suspicion but the alibi provided by his daughter, plus Travers's horrified insistance that the Yeti must be found, convinced the Police of his innocence. The murder was never solved, the Yeti never found.

In the weeks that followed, the story was driven from the headlines by an even stranger mystery. Patches of mist began to appear in Central London. Unlike any natural mist, they refused to disperse. More and more patches appeared, linking up one with another. Most terrifying of all, people who spent any time in the mist patches were found dead, their faces covered with cobwebs. Central London was cordoned off. It was still possible to travel by Underground Railway—until a strange cobweb-like substance started to spread below ground, completely blocking the tunnels. It was like a glowing mist made solid, and anyone who entered it was never seen again. The combination of mist above and cobweb below became known as the Web. Slowly it spread.

Then the Yeti reappeared, not just one but hordes of them, roaming through the misty streets and the cobwebbed tunnels, mercilessly killing anyone in their path. Central London was gripped tight in a Web of Fear...

# 2

## The Web in Space

Inside the control room of that mysterious Space/
Time craft known as the TARDIS, a furious argument
was raging between two very different figures. One
was a small man with untidy black hair and a gentle,
humorous face. He wore baggy check trousers and a
disreputable old frock-coat. Towering over him was a
brawny youth in Highland dress, complete with kilt.
The smaller man was that well-known traveller in
Space and Time called the Doctor. The other, whose
name was Jamie, had been the Doctor's travelling
companion since the Doctor's visit to Earth at the time
of the Jacobite rebellion.

Usually the two were the best of friends. However,
occasional disputes were inevitable, and this one
concerned Jamie's duties as the Doctor's assistant.
Largely to keep him occupied, the Doctor had
given Jamie one or two simple tasks concerned with
the running of the TARDIS. The fact that Jamie
was completely lacking in technological knowledge

made him all the more determined to carry them out correctly.

'Now see here, Doctor,' he said stubbornly. 'You told me to watch that control panel and warn you if yon light flashed. Well, it flashed!' Jamie folded his arms defiantly.

The Doctor tried to be patient. 'If that light had flashed it would mean we've landed. And we're still travelling.'

'Aye, well that's as mebbe. But I know what I saw— and yon light flashed!'

'Oh really, Jamie...'

They were interrupted by the opening of the door from the TARDIS's living quarters. A small, dark girl entered the control room. Her name was Victoria, and she was the Doctor's other travelling companion. Rescued from nineteenth-century London during a terrifying adventure with the Daleks, Victoria had joined the Doctor and Jamie in their travels. Usually she wore the long, flowing dresses of her own age, but they were cumbersome and impractical during the strenuously active adventures in which the Doctor tended to involve her. Rummaging through the TARDIS clothing lockers, Victoria had found a jacket and slacks small enough to fit her. Now, greatly daring, she was wearing the outfit for the first time. Hopefully she looked at Jamie. 'Do you like it?'

'Like what?'

'I found these clothes in the locker. I think they suit me, don't you?'

The Doctor smiled. 'Very much. Don't you agree, Jamie?'

Jamie glanced briefly at Victoria and said, 'Aye, verra nice. Now then, Doctor, I'm no daft—I saw what I saw.'

Victoria was staring over their shoulder, 'Why's that light flashing?' she asked innocently.

The Doctor spun round, but the flashing had stopped. 'Are you two having a game with me?'

Jamie grinned at Victoria. 'You see? He willna' listen!'

The Doctor was peering at the control console. The movement of the central column was slowing down. 'Well, bless my soul,' he said. 'We appear to be landing!' His hands flickered over the switches as he checked the automatic landing procedure. 'All seems to be going smoothly. Let's find out where we are.'

The Doctor switched on the scanner. He saw only the blackness of space, broken by a scattering of stars.

Victoria could tell he was worried. 'What's happened?'

'Something very strange. We're out of the Space/Time Vortex—but we're suspended in Space!' The Doctor began running a series of rapid checks muttering to himself, 'Gravity off, power on, control on, flight on...'

Jamie watched him gloomily. 'Ye dinna make sense. We've landed, and yet we havna' landed?'

Victoria peered at the scanner. A curious, cobwebby growth was creeping over the screen, a kind of solid mist. 'Look, Doctor. It's like a spider's web.'

The Doctor looked. 'Fascinating. That's what's holding us here—but why?' He gazed at the scanner, lost in thought.

Angrily Jamie burst out, 'Well, dinna' just stand there, Doctor. Do something!'

The Doctor seemed to come to. He beamed at Jamie. 'Practical as ever, my boy. And quite right too.' The Doctor opened a locker and began rummaging inside. He produced a small red box, blew a layer of dust off it, then fished out an electronic tool kit. Fingers working rapidly, the Doctor began wiring the box into the console, while Victoria and Jamie looked on.

'What's the box for, Doctor?' asked Victoria.

The Doctor went on working. 'It's a power-booster.' He pointed to a button in the lid. 'When I press this, the total power of the TARDIS will be channelled into one massive surge. It should be enough to wrench us free from whatever's holding us, and set us down somewhere else. That is *if* everything goes to plan.'

'And if it doesn't?'

'The TARDIS will probably blow up,' the Doctor said cheerfully. He finished his work, snapped shut the lid of the box and looked at them. 'Ready everybody? Then hold tight!'

Jamie and Victoria took a firm grip of the edge of the central console, and the Doctor pressed the button. There was a sudden crescendo of electronic noise as the central column began to move again, slowly at first then with increasing speed. With a final shriek of power, the TARDIS jerked, vibrated and spun. The Doctor and his companions were sent flying across the control room. Then the noise and movement cut out. Everything was quiet and still.

The Doctor struggled to his feet, and went to the control console. Jamie helped Victoria to her feet. Both were shaken and bruised but otherwise unhurt. The Doctor glanced up from his instruments. 'Well, it worked. We've landed, really landed this time.'

'I don't suppose you ken where,' asked Jamie. 'Or *when* either?'

The Doctor shook his head. 'I'm afraid the readings are a bit erratic.' He patted the console affectionately. 'The poor old girl's somewhat shaken up.'

'What are we going to do now?' asked Victoria.

The Doctor rubbed his chin. 'It's too soon to take off. We've eluded our captor for the moment, but I don't want to get stuck in that Web again. Let's see where we've landed.' He adjusted controls on the scanner. They saw darkness, and the vague shape of an arched roof. 'We seem to be inside somewhere. I've a feeling we're underground.' He peered at the instruments again. 'The atmosphere gauge seems to be working. There's air out there... Suppose we take a look?'

Jamie moved eagerly towards the doors. Victoria hung back.

'Do you think it's safe?'

'I shouldn't think so for a moment!' Smiling in happy anticipation, the Doctor operated the TARDIS doors. They opened to reveal—nothing. Just sinister blackness. 'Hold on,' said the Doctor. 'We'll be needing these.' He opened a wall-locker and produced a couple of large torches, handing one to Jamie and keeping the other himself. Switching on the torches, they left the TARDIS.

The air outside was dank and chill, a curious dead feel to it. The Doctor locked the door of the TARDIS, which looked from the outside like an old Police Box. He swept the beam of his torch around. It revealed a long, tiled corridor with an arched roof. Jamie pointed his torch in the other direction.

'There's an opening along here, Doctor. Seems to be steps, leading down.' Eagerly Jamie ran forward. The others followed, Victoria taking care to keep close to the Doctor.

'If there are steps they must lead somewhere,' the Doctor agreed. 'Come on.'

The steps took them down and down through the darkness. Victoria wondered what lay before them this time. Perhaps they were in the lair of an underground monster. Jamie ranged eagerly ahead, and Victoria could see his torch bobbing about below them. His voice floated up. 'I've come to the end of the steps. There's another arch—seems to give onto a kind of long tunnel.'

'Hold on, Jamie,' called the Doctor. 'We're coming.' He took Victoria's hand and led her down the steps. Shining his torch ahead, the Doctor guided them cautiously through the arch.

Victoria looked around in astonishment. The arch led through a short passageway which was at right angles to a long tunnel with tiled walls and a curved ceiling. They were standing on a raised platform which ran parallel to the tunnel. Where the platform ended the tunnel narrowed, and disappeared into darkness. Turning round, Victoria saw that the same thing happened at the other end. The walls of the tunnel were papered with brightly covered notices. They were written in English, but Victoria couldn't make much sense of them.

Jamie looked round inquisitively. 'Why does the floor drop away like that?'

'Be careful, Jamie, don't go too close,' the Doctor warned.

In the glow of the Doctor's torch Victoria saw a big notice on the wall behind her—and this was something she could understand. 'Doctor—look,' she called. The Doctor swept his torch over the notice. Slowly Victoria read out loud. 'It says "Covent Garden".'

Jamie was unimpressed. 'Oh aye? And what's that?'

'It's a market,' said Victoria excitedly. 'A place where they sell vegetables and fruit and flowers...'

Jamie looked round and sniffed. 'Funny sort of a market.'

The Doctor smiled. 'We're not at the market,' he explained. 'Though we must be very near it. We're in an Underground Station.'

'A station,' said Victoria incredulously. 'Trains? Here? What about all the steam and smoke?'

'These are electric trains. A bit after your time, Victoria—and a long way after Jamie's.' Briefly the Doctor explained the workings of London's Underground Railway system. Jamie was used to scientific marvels since he'd started travelling with the Doctor. To him a train was like a spaceship—just another of the future wonders he took for granted. But his practical mind was quick to spot a flaw in the Doctor's explanation.

'If this place is a station, why's it all dark and empty?'

'Probably the middle of the night,' the Doctor answered cheerfully. 'Let's go up top. There'll be plenty of activity there.'

A long climb up interminable flights of stairs brought them puffing and exhausted into a silent and empty ticket hall. The Doctor looked round at the abandoned ticket-collector's booth, the deserted ticket machines. There wasn't a soul in sight. An iron grille was drawn across the station entrance. Outside in the street it was daylight. Rather a strange kind of daylight though. It had a pearly shimmering quality, and wisps of mist seemed to hang motionless in the air.

Jamie crossed to the metal grille and tried to open it, but it was shut fast. 'Looks as though we're locked in.'

The Doctor frowned. 'It's all very strange,' he admitted.

'Listen!' said Victoria.

They listened. After a moment Jamie spoke, 'I canna hear a thing.'

'Exactly,' said Victoria triumphantly. 'And Covent Garden is right in the middle of London!'

Jamie was peering through the iron grille. 'Look, Doctor, there's someone here!' Huddled against the station door was a newspaper seller, apparently dozing beside his small news-stand. Jamie stretched an arm through the grille and tapped him on the shoulder. 'Hey, mister, could you tell us what's going on?' The man made no reply. Jamie shook him by the shoulder. The huddled shape rolled over backwards, landing at their feet. Victoria jumped back and screamed. The still, dead face was covered with filmy grey cobwebs.

'Do you see that?' demanded Jamie. 'Just like that stuff on the scanner.'

The Doctor looked through the grille. The falling of the body had revealed a placard on the news-stand. In huge capital letters it screamed, 'KILLER MIST PANIC—LONDONERS FLEE!'

# 3

## The Monster in the Tunnels

The Doctor led them away from the grille, across the ticket hall and back down the stairs. Now as they descended, Victoria asked, 'What are we going to do, go back to the TARDIS?'

'No point. If I took off again we could easily find ourselves trapped in that Web. The power-boost might not work a second time. Anyway, I'm convinced that what's happening in London is connected to what happened to us. We've got to find out what's going on, if only for our own safety.'

'Then where *are* we going?' Victoria realised the Doctor had already made his plan. As usual, he just hadn't bothered to tell them about it.

'Didn't I tell you? We're going to make our way through the tunnels to another station, reach the surface that way.'

'If we want to reach the surface, why don't we just bash down yon grille?' Jamie was always in favour of the direct solution.

'Because I don't want to reach *that* surface,' said the Doctor irritably. 'This station is in the heart of all the trouble. We don't want to end up like that poor newspaper man. We'll go through the tunnels till we reach a station that's open, with people about to tell us what's happening.'

By now they'd arrived back on the platform, and before the Doctor could stop him, Jamie had vaulted down on to the track.

'Don't move!' yelled the Doctor. 'Whatever you do, don't touch those rails.'

Jamie froze, one foot in the air. The Doctor jumped down beside him, took a tiny meter from his pocket and touched it gingerly to one of the rails. The needle on the dial didn't even flicker, and the Doctor sighed with relief. 'All right, Jamie, the electricity's off. You can relax.'

Jamie lowered his foot. 'What was all the fuss about?'

'I told you these were electric trains,' said the Doctor reprovingly. 'If there'd been current in those rails, you'd be dead by now.'

The Doctor helped Victoria down on to the track. 'We should be safe enough. Better not touch the rails though, someone might switch on again!' Walking carefully between the rails they set off along the tunnel. Suddenly the Doctor stooped and ran a finger along the rail.

'I thought you said don't touch,' Victoria looked at him in the darkness.

20

The Doctor held up his finger. It was covered in dust. 'Just confirming a theory. These rails haven't been used for some time.'

They continued along the tunnel, lighting their way with the torches. Jamie as usual was pushing ahead. 'Hey, look at this!' he called, shining his torch. They had reached a junction where the tunnel split in two, forming the shape of a capital Y. In the centre of the junction stood a heavy drum of electrical cable. A length of cable led from it into the left-hand tunnel, disappearing into the darkness. The drum was nearly empty.

The Doctor examined it thoughtfully. 'Now how long has that been here?' He ran his finger along the top. There was no dust.

With eerie suddenness a row of dim working-lights came on in the tunnel. The three companions looked at each other in alarm. They heard footsteps moving towards them from the left-hand tunnel. 'Quick,' whispered the Doctor. 'Hide!' He led them into an alcove. They waited silently. The heavy crunch of booted feet came steadily nearer. Three soldiers appeared, submachine-guns slung over their shoulders, all glancing around with continual wariness. Two were carrying a full drum of cable between them, on a pole thrust through its centre. The third lifted the nearly-empty drum and they set off down the right-hand tunnel, the third man paying out cable behind him.

The Doctor stared after the soldiers. 'I wonder what they're doing down here?'

Jamie snorted. 'You could always have popped out and asked them!'

'And get shot by accident?' The Doctor shook his head. 'Those men were in a mood to shoot anything that moved. Even if they didn't fire at us, they'd probably have locked us up somewhere on general suspicion. I think we ought to tread very carefully till we know what's going on.'

Jamie nodded, remembering the wary tenseness of the soldiers. 'Aye, mebbe you're right. So what do we do?'

'You and Victoria follow the soldiers, but keep your distance. I want to find out what's at the other end of this wire. We'll all meet back here in about fifteen minutes.'

'Right.' Taking Victoria by the hand Jamie led her off after the soldiers. The Doctor began moving down the left-hand tunnel, following the course of the wire.

The two soldiers carrying the full drum were Corporal Blake and Private Weams. The one with the nearly-empty drum was a tough old sweat called Sergeant Arnold. Suddenly Weams stopped, causing Blake to stop as well. 'What's the matter?'

Weams was the youngest and most nervous of the three. 'Thought I heard something, Corp.'

They all listened. Arnold said threateningly, 'Getting a bit jumpy, aren't you, lad?' Although Arnold was a kindly man, he hated anyone to know it, and always spoke with the ferocity of a drill-sergeant on the barrack square.

Weams flushed. 'No wonder if I am, is it, Sarge?'

Before the Sergeant could reply, Corporal Blake cut in diplomatically, 'You're almost out of cable, Sarge. Shall I connect up the new drum?' Arnold nodded, passing his drum over, and the Corporal set to work.

Further down the tunnel, hidden by its curve, Jamie gave Victoria's arm a warning squeeze. 'They've stopped moving. I can hear them talking. We'll just have to wait.'

Victoria nodded meekly. In a very small voice she whispered, 'Oh Jamie, I don't like it down here.'

Meanwhile Sergeant Arnold was saying, 'So you don't like it down here, eh lad. Well, neither do I and nor does Corporal Blake. But it's a job, and it has to be done.'

Weams nodded. 'You reckon this'll work, Sarge?'

'Course it'll work, won't it, Corporal?'

Blake didn't answer. Arnold leaned over him and hissed in his ear. 'Corporal Blake!'

'Sorry, Sarge, I was listening.'

'Then you should have heard me talking to you,' said Arnold in a blood-curdling whisper.

Behind them in the tunnel Jamie whispered, 'Seems to have gone quiet, I think they've moved on. We'll give it a minute or two and then follow.'

23

Victoria moved closer to him. Something silky brushed her face. She gave a scream, stifling it with her hand.

Further up the tunnel, the listening soldiers looked at each other. Sergeant Arnold unslung his submachine-gun, slipped off the safety catch and moved cautiously back down the tunnel.

Jamie and Victoria were flattened against the wall, Victoria brushing frantically at her hair. Jamie looked at her reproachfully, 'Och girl, it's only a wee spider's web.'

'I'm sorry, Jamie. Do you think they heard?'

'Well, mebbe not. All seems quiet again. Come on.'

They moved along the tunnel. As they rounded the curve the soldiers were nowhere in sight. Jamie turned to Victoria. 'They must be well ahead by now. We'd better catch up.'

Suddenly two soldiers came running down the tunnel, guns at the ready. Jamie and Victoria turned to flee, but Sergeant Arnold stepped from an alcove behind them. 'Well, would you believe it? The Babes in the Wood!' His submachine-gun was aimed at a point exactly between them. Jamie and Victoria raised their hands.

Harold Chorley touched the controls of his tape recorder and spoke in the deep, mellow tones he reserved for his professional moments. 'And finally, Captain Knight, how would you sum up your personal feelings about your late Commanding Officer?'

The tall young officer on the other side of the table had none of Chorley's polished smoothness. His voice was awkward and almost painfully sincere as he replied, 'Er... well... Colonel Pemberton was a very brave man, no doubt about that. He gave his life for his country. I'm proud to have served under him.'

Chorley switched off the recorder and Knight looked uncertain. 'That all right?'

Chorley nodded. 'Sterling stuff, Captain. You talk in quotes.'

There was an edge to Captain Knight's voice as he replied, 'Not just quotes. I happen to mean it.'

Chorley smiled vaguely, but said nothing. He was an impressive-looking man with a stern, handsome face, and a deep, melodious voice. He was also extremely photogenic. On television he gave the impression of a sincere, wise and responsible man. Unfortunately, his looks were deceptive. Chorley was weak, vain and in reality rather stupid. But appearances count for a great deal in public life. Chorley's voice and his looks, together with a certain natural cunning, had enabled him to establish himself as one of television's best-known interviewers and reporters. He had one other useful attribute for success—he was extremely lucky. Chorley happened to be on the spot when the present crisis broke. He had deftly persuaded an impressionable Government official that he was the one man best able to handle official coverage—much to the disgust of his colleagues.

As Knight moved away, Chorley, quite unabashed, switched on his tape recorder and began to speak. 'That was an interview with Captain Knight, the young officer temporarily in command of the Special Unit after the tragic death of his commanding officer, Colonel Pemberton, in a Yeti attack!' Chorley paused, collecting his thoughts. 'I am speaking to you from the Operations Room. I am now in the very heart of the Underground Fortress close to Goodge Street Station. Built as a secret Government H.Q. during World War Two, the Fortress has been reactivated to become the home of the Special Unit, the mixed military and scientific force set up to look for an answer to the crisis that has turned Central London into a desert of fear.' Pleased with this last phrase Chorley looked round the room. 'This Control Room, empty for over thirty years, is now packed with the most modern electronic, scientific and communications equipment. An illuminated map shows the whole of the London Tube System. Other parts of the Fortress contain rest and recreation rooms, sleeping quarters, a canteen and fully equipped kitchen, as well as a special laboratory in which one of the country's leading scientists toils night and day to find an answer to the terror that moves steadily closer.'

Temporarily drying up, Chorley switched off and glanced hopefully round for more 'copy'. On the other side of the room, Captain Knight stood by an elaborate communications set-up, peering over the shoulder of Corporal Lane, as the young corporal spoke into his mike. 'Hullo, hullo. I say again, do you read me?' Lane looked up worriedly. 'No good, can't raise 'em, sir.'

Knight looked at his watch. 'That supply truck was due twenty minutes ago.'

Lane did his best to sound cheerful. 'Wouldn't worry, sir. Could be just a breakdown. We've never had trouble at Holborn before.'

Knight nodded. 'I hope you're right, Corporal. Keep on trying.'

He turned away from the set as the burly figure of Professor Travers bustled into the room. 'There you are, Knight. That blast-meter working properly yet?'

'Your daughter's checking it over now, sir.'

Travers grunted. 'She'd better get a move on. Must be able to measure the extent of the explosion.'

On the other side of the room, Harold Chorley saw his opportunity, and switched on the recorder. 'I'm just about to have a word with Professor Edward Travers. Together with his daughter Anne, herself a distinguished scientist, he is responsible for the scientific side of things here.' Clutching his recorder Chorley crossed the room. 'Professor Travers,' he began accusingly. 'So far you don't seem to be having much success. How long do you think it will take you to come up with an answer?'

Travers, busily studying a row of complex dials, answered only with a grunt.

Unwisely, Chorley pressed on. 'A week perhaps? Two weeks? Three weeks?'

Travers swung round. 'It is more than likely that we shall be unable to defeat this menace at all,' he rumbled. 'In which case London, perhaps the whole of England, will be completely wiped out.'

Hastily Chorley switched off the recorder. 'Really, Professor!' he spluttered.

An attractive young woman came into the Operations Room, a complex piece of equipment in her hand. Forgetting Chorley at once, Travers turned to her, 'There you are, Anne. That blast-meter working?'

She nodded. 'I'll just wire it into the circuit.'

'Let me help you,' said Captain Knight hurriedly. He could easily have sent for a technician, but he welcomed any opportunity to work with Anne Travers.

Anne smiled. 'It's all right, Captain,' she said gently. 'I can manage.'

Travers hurried out saying, 'I'll be in my lab. Let me know how things go!'

Anne moved towards a separate console of instruments in one corner. The panel was dominated by a large clock, and a red firing-button. Knight followed her and Chorley bustled across after them. 'Captain Knight, I'm afraid I must protest. Professor Travers is being both obstructive and secretive. Miss Travers, perhaps you can help me?'

Anne had already started working. 'I'm afraid I'm a little busy at the moment.'

Chorley was outraged. Usually people fell over themselves to talk to him. 'I must insist. The public has a right to be informed...' He broke off as Captain Knight took his arm in a painful grip and led him towards the door.

'I'm afraid Miss Travers is too busy to talk at the moment, Mr Chorley,' said Knight with steely politeness. 'We're approaching an important part of our operation.'

Chorley freed his arm with an angry jerk. 'You might at least tell me what you're doing.'

'Very well, Mr Chorley, if it will keep you quiet. We are planning to destroy certain areas of the Tube System to stem the advance of the Web. We are just about to blow up Charing Cross Station.'

The Doctor followed the trail of wire cable for what seemed an interminably long way. At last the tunnel opened out on to a station platform. Emergency lights glowed dimly. The Doctor peered at the sign on the wall. It read, 'Charing Cross'.

The wire left the tracks and ran up on to the platform. It ended in a small metal box, which stood at the foot of a pile of wooden crates. The Doctor realised that the wire led not to a communications network as he'd hoped, but to the detonating device for an extremely large pile of high explosive. He was about to climb on to the platform for a closer look, when he heard the sound of a heavy step. Hurriedly the Doctor ducked down below platform level. The steps came nearer and nearer. Then silence. Slowly the Doctor raised his head.

He saw two huge clawed, furry feet, and quickly dropped down again, craning his head back at the same time. He already knew what he would see. Towering over him was the giant form of a Yeti.

# 4

## Danger for the Doctor

The Yeti's feet were inches from the Doctor's head, but luckily for the Doctor the creature didn't look down. Instead it moved away across the platform. After a few moments the Doctor risked a cautious peep, and saw that the Yeti was standing by the pile of explosives. A second Yeti appeared from the shadows of the platform arch. Flanking the pile of crates, the two Yeti stood as if on guard.

For quite some time nothing happened. The Doctor waited. It would be dangerous to move with the Yeti so close, and anyhow he wanted to see what they were up to. More precisely he wanted to discover the plans of the Great Intelligence which controlled them. The Yeti themselves were no more than mindless robots, controlled by impulses picked up by the sphere nestling in their chest units.

Incongruous as they were, in the setting of the London Underground, the Doctor felt no great surprise at seeing the Yeti again. Ever since that mysterious Web had held the TARDIS suspended in space, the Doctor had suspected that the Great Intelligence had returned to attack him. Exiled from some other dimension, the Intelligence was a malignant disembodied entity, condemned to hover eternally between the stars, forever craving form and substance. It possessed the power to take over human servants, who became totally subservient to its will, their own personalities utterly swallowed up. Yeti provided the brute strength and terror, human puppets supervised and controlled their actions. That was how the Great Intelligence had operated in Tibet, and the Doctor felt sure the same pattern would be repeated.*

The electronic bleeping of a Yeti signal broke in on his reflections. It came from the darkness of the tunnel. The Yeti guarding the explosives answered the signal, then a third Yeti appeared, holding a squat, broad-barrelled device shaped like a gun. It made straight for the pile of crates, and the other two moved to make way for it. The Yeti aimed the device at the crates and fired. A fine mist came from the barrel and the Doctor saw thick cobwebs beginning to form on the boxes...

In the Operations Room, Anne Travers was completing her final checks, Captain Knight still standing beside her. Watching the slim fingers as they

*See 'Doctor Who and the Abominable Snowmen'

deftly checked terminals and connections, Knight said, 'What's a nice girl like you—'

'Doing in a place like this?' Anne smiled as she completed the old cliché for him. 'When I was a little girl I decided I'd like to become a scientist like my father. So I did.'

'Just like that?'

'Just like that.'

Sergeant Arnold flung open the door, marched across the room and crashed to attention in front of Captain Knight, throwing up a quivering salute. 'Sir!' he bellowed.

Knight returned the salute. 'So there you are, Sergeant. You've been quite a time. Any trouble?'

'Not what you'd call trouble, sir, but—'

'Is the cable connected?' interrupted Knight. 'Where's the other end?'

'Cable connected as ordered, sir,' roared the Sergeant. 'Lads are bringing it in now—hurry up, you dozy lot, chop chop!'

Weams and Blake walked in paying out cable as they came. They were followed by Chorley, who used their entrance as an opportunity to slip back into the Operations Room. He looked on as the two soldiers began wiring the cable in the control console. 'Isn't all this a little primitive?' he demanded. 'Surely you could use something radio-controlled?'

'We tried that,' said Knight patiently.

'And?'

'No use. Some force in the tunnels prevented the detonating signal from being transmitted. So we've returned to the old-fashioned method. It may be primitive—but it'll work.' Knight turned back to Sergeant Arnold, who was obviously bursting to speak. 'All right, Sergeant, what is it?'

'We found a couple of youngsters, sir, boy and a girl. Wandering about in the tunnel, refused to give a proper account of themselves. I've got 'em in the Common Room under guard. Thought you'd want to see them, sir.'

'Oh blast,' Knight said irritably. 'Well I can't be bothered with them now. This demolition job's overdue as it is.'

Anne looked up from her work. 'You're sure there were only two of them?'

'Two's all we found, miss. Why?'

'That whole area was supposed to be cleared. I don't like the idea of blowing up the station if there are people wandering around.'

'There's still a few minutes to detonation,' Knight pointed out. 'Better have a word with them, Sergeant, make sure there was no one else with them.'

'Sir!' Arnold saluted and marched out.

Jamie and Victoria were waiting in the Common Room, an armed sentry at the door. It was a largish room with armchairs and tables scattered about. Heaps of old magazines lay on the tables, there was a darts board, a couple of chess sets, even a table tennis table. A trestle table in the corner held a tea urn and some thick, chipped mugs.

Jamie scowled at the sentry and whispered to Victoria, 'The Doctor was right, ye ken. First thing they do is lock us both up.'

Victoria looked round. 'Well at least we're not in a cell. And they don't seem too unfriendly.'

'I dinna trust them,' Jamie muttered darkly. 'They're just trying to win us over.'

Sergeant Arnold came into the room, his tough, craggy features fixed in a smile. 'Looking after you, are they?' he began heartily. 'How about a cuppa?' He filled two mugs from the tea urn and passed them over.

'How long are you keeping us here?' Jamie sounded truculent.

'Till the officer's got time to see you, that's all.'

'What is this place anyway?' Victoria asked. 'And what are you all doing down here?'

Arnold gave her a reproving look. 'Ah now, Miss, everyone knows what's been happening. You shouldn't have come down into these tunnels.' Victoria started to speak but Arnold held up his hand. 'Not so many questions, if you don't mind. You're here to answer questions, not ask 'em. To begin with, were you on your own?'

Jamie looked doubtfully at him. 'Why do you ask?'

'Because I want to know, lad. Now—was there anyone with you?'

Jamie and Victoria glanced at each other. Again Victoria started to speak. This time it was Jamie who interrupted her. 'No,' he said firmly.

'You're sure of that?'

'Aye, I'm sure.' Jamie was determined not to give the Doctor away. If he told these soldiers about him, they'd send men straight out to find him. Then the Doctor would be locked up too, which was just what he didn't want.

Sergeant Arnold looked up as Captain Knight popped his head round the door. 'We're all ready, Sergeant.' He looked enquiringly at Jamie and Victoria. 'On their own, were they?'

'Yessir.'

'Jolly good.' Captain Knight disappeared.

Jamie looked after him. 'What was all that about?'

Arnold poured himself a mug of tea. 'Lucky for you we found you, my lad. We're just about to blow up some of those tunnels.'

Captain Knight strode into the Operations Room and nodded to Corporal Lane. 'It's all right, apparently, they were on their own. Carry out final checks, fire when ready.'

The Doctor watched while the Yeti completed its strange task. Soon the entire pile of crates was cocooned in the cobwebby substance. The Yeti lowered the Web-gun and stepped back. It turned and marched off, the other two Yeti close behind.

The Doctor waited until they were gone, then clambered up on the platform. He went over to the cobwebbed crates and began examining them curiously.

Corporal Lane looked across the Operations Room to Captain Knight. 'Firing checks complete, sir. Ready to detonate.'

'Carry on, Corporal.'

Lane's thumb came down on the red button.

The Doctor was gingerly rubbing the cobweb-substance between his fingers. There came a muffled thump, a blinding white flash, and everything went dark...

Just as Lane pressed the firing button, Sergeant Arnold ran into the Operations Room. 'Don't detonate, sir!' he called, then stopped, realising he was too late. As Knight swung round in astonishment Arnold went on, 'Those kids have changed their story, sir. There *was* someone else with them—some kind of a Doctor.'

'What! If he was anywhere near those explosives...'

'I think he must have been, sir. Apparently he was following the cable.'

Captain Knight sighed. 'All right, Sergeant. Take a party and see what you can find.'

As Arnold saluted and left, Corporal Lane called out, 'Blast recorder doesn't seem to be working, sir.'

'Rubbish. Miss Travers has just checked it.'

'Nothing registering, sir.'

Anne crossed over to the console and examined the dials. 'I'm afraid he's right.' She moved to another set of dials and frowned. 'But the circuit checks show there *was* an explosion.'

Knight sounded exasperated. 'You can't have an explosion without blast—can you?'

Anne shook her head.

Knight scowled, 'This Doctor who was in the tunnels—maybe he tampered with the charge. I think I'll have a chat with those two youngsters.'

He strode along the corridor to the Common Room. Anne followed. Chorley, ever alert for a story, tagged along behind clutching his tape recorder.

As soon as they entered the room Jamie and Victoria jumped up with a flood of questions. Knight stopped them. 'Quiet both of you. And sit down.' Victoria and Jamie sat, fearing the worst. More gently Knight went on, 'We've no news of your friend as yet. We've sent someone to investigate. Meanwhile, I want to know exactly what you were doing in the tunnels.'

Jamie and Victoria looked at each other, faced not for the first time with explaining their presence in some unauthorised place. The TARDIS never seemed to put them down anywhere safe.

When they didn't answer, Chorley spoke up, eager to use his skill as an interrogator. 'Where did you break into the Underground System?'

Jamie glared indignantly at him. 'We didna' break in anywhere.'

'You must have done,' snapped Chorley triumphantly. 'All the stations are sealed off, aren't they? How else could you get here?'

Jamie looked helplessly at Victoria, who said weakly, 'We just—arrived. We were brought here.'

'By this mysterious Doctor? And for what purpose? Was it sabotage?' Chorley was well in his stride by now.

'Och no,' said Jamie bewildered. 'You're making it all sound far worse than it is.'

Private Weams appeared in the doorway. 'Excuse me, sir, Corporal's raised Holborn on the radio. Sounds like trouble—another Yeti attack!'

Forgetting Jamie and Victoria, Knight ran from the room, Chorley at his heels. Jamie stared after them, 'Did yon soldier say Yeti? Those robot things we had so much trouble with in Tibet?'

Victoria nodded. 'I think so.'

'Och no, not again! Trust the Doctor.'

Victoria made a shushing gesture, but it was too late. Anne Travers had paused in the doorway and was studying them keenly. 'All right, you two,' she said determinedly. 'Just how do you know so much about the Yeti?'

*

In the Operations Room, Knight stood over Corporal Lane, who was talking into his communications setup. 'Hullo, Holborn, do you read me... Fortress H.Q. to Holborn.' He looked up. 'Sorry, sir. Seem to have lost them again.' He listened to the faint noise coming from his earphones. 'I can hear something, sir. Sounds like firing.'

'Full amplification,' ordered Knight. 'Put it on loudspeaker.' Lane adjusted controls and flicked a switch. The room was filled with the crackling of static, mixed with the sound of gunfire. There were shouts and screams. Suddenly, full blast, there came the nerve-shattering roar of a Yeti—then silence. Lane tried the controls, then shook his head.

'Nothing, sir. They're no longer transmitting.' There was a moment's silence. Everyone realised what must have happened.

Captain Knight said, 'You *were* talking to them—before?'

'Just a few words, sir, very faint. Far as I could gather the ammo truck had trouble on the way, and arrived very late. They must have got the ammo unloaded, sir, they were just leaving when they were attacked...'

'I'll take a squad myself and have a look. We've got to have that ammunition.'

Corporal Lane added, 'I'd like to volunteer, sir. That other radio operator was a mate of mine.'

'All right. Private Weams, take over from the Corporal.'

As he turned to go Knight noticed Chorley. He had been recording the last moments of the Holborn squad on his tape recorder.

'Splendid stuff that, Captain. Most dramatic. Lots of action.'

Knight stopped. 'We're going to see what happened to those men, Mr Chorley. Perhaps you'd like to come with us. You might see some "action" at first hand.'

Chorley recoiled. 'Er, yes, well...most kind, but I wouldn't want to get in your way. Perhaps I'd better stay here.'

'Yes,' Knight said contemptuously. 'Perhaps you'd better.' Followed by Corporal Lane he strode out of the room.

Sergeant Arnold and Corporal Blake stood examining a cobwebbed pile of shattered wood—all that remained of several crates of high explosive. Arnold raked among the debris and picked out a few fragments of twisted metal. 'What do you make of this?'

'Part of our detonator. So it fired all right. But if it went off...'

'Why didn't the tunnel come down? Why's all this wood piled together instead of scattered around? How can you have an explosion without any damage?'

41

'Obvious, innit?' said Blake. 'Someone interfered with the charge. Maybe this Doctor bloke.'

Arnold nodded. 'Maybe. I'd certainly like to know where he is!'

The Doctor woke from a nightmare in which he was running furiously through endless semi-darkness—only to find that the nightmare was true. He forced himself to stop, and leaned gasping against the tunnel wall, while he tried to remember what had happened.

The explosives had gone off while he was examining them. But there had been no explosion, not in the true sense. The cobweb cocoon with which the Yeti had covered the boxes had somehow absorbed all the power. But the Doctor had been standing only inches away, and enough explosive energy had remained to send him flying across the platform. He could dimly remember picking himself up and running frantically into the tunnels, presumably in a mild state of shell-shock.

Now more or less himself, the Doctor realised he had no idea how long he'd been running or in what direction. He might even have passed through other stations in his headlong flight. How on earth was he going to find Jamie and Victoria? They couldn't be left to roam the tunnels, not with Yeti on the loose again. The Doctor groped in his pocket, looking to see if his torch had survived unbroken. It hadn't and he threw it away. Suddenly a light-beam flashed out of the semi-darkness and a clipped voice spoke. 'Stand perfectly still and raise your hands.'

The Doctor obeyed. A tall figure appeared, torch in one hand, revolver in the other, covering the Doctor. It was a man in battledress, the insignia of a Colonel on his shoulders. Even through the semi-darkness the Doctor caught an impression of an immaculate uniform and a neatly trimmed moustache. The soldier peered down from his superior height at the small, scruffy figure of his captive. 'And who might you be?' he asked, sounding more amused than alarmed.

Feeling at something of a disadvantage the Doctor answered sulkily, 'I might ask you the same question.'

'I am Colonel Alistair Lethbridge-Stewart,' said the precise, military voice.

'How do you do? I am the Doctor.'

'Are you now? Well then, Doctor whoever-you-are, perhaps you'd like to tell me what you're doing in these tunnels?'

# 5

## Battle with the Yeti

Although neither of them realised it, this was in its way as historic an encounter as that between Stanley and Doctor Livingstone. Promoted to Brigadier, Lethbridge-Stewart would one day lead the British section of an organisation called UNIT (United Nations Intelligence Taskforce), set up to fight alien attacks on the planet Earth. The Doctor, changed in appearance and temporarily exiled to Earth, was to become UNIT's Scientific Adviser.* But that was all in the future. For the moment the two friends-to-be glared at each other in mutual suspicion.

'Never mind how I got here,' said the Doctor impatiently. 'You wouldn't believe me if I told you. The important thing is that there are Yeti in these tunnels. They're robot servants of an alien entity called the Great Intelligence. We must warn the Authorities at once.'

*See 'Doctor Who and the Auton Invasion'

Lethbridge-Stewart's revolver, which he had lowered on seeing the Doctor's harmless appearance, was raised to cover him once more. 'The Authorities already know about the Yeti, Doctor. But not, it seems, as much as you do. I think you'd better come with me.'

Professor Travers's laboratory had originally been an army workshop. Now the heavy machinery had been cleared away and the benches were loaded with a complex array of electronic equipment. Travers was hard at work. Having discovered, more or less by accident, how to activate a control sphere, he was now reversing the direction of his researches, and trying to find a means of jamming these inside the Yeti. If he could manage this, he would be able to render the Yeti harmless.

Absorbed in his work he didn't notice his daughter Anne come in. She had to speak twice before he looked up and grunted, 'What is it? You can see I'm busy.' Suddenly he remembered. 'Oh yes. How did the demolition go?'

'Apparently it didn't! Captain Knight has sent some men to investigate. I didn't come about that, Father. The soldiers found two youngsters in the tunnels. I've just been talking to them. They seem to know a great deal about the Yeti. They know they're robots, they know about the control spheres. And they talked about something called the Intelligence, which first appeared in Tibet.'

Travers put down the control sphere he was working on. 'I think you'd better take me to see them.'

Jamie and Victoria stood up as Anne and Travers came into the Common Room. Travers didn't speak. He just stood staring in utter disbelief. A small dark girl and a boy in Highland dress. The Doctor's two companions—Travers remembered meeting them on the snowy mountain path outside Det-Sen Monastery, remembered the incredible adventures they had shared. Now they were here, over forty years later—but looking exactly the same.

Jamie and Victoria looked curiously at the white-bearded old man who was staring at them so strangely. Victoria stared back, then a strange feeling of familiarity came over her. Beneath the white whiskers, the mop of white hair and the wrinkles of age, she could recognise a familiar face. 'It's Mr Travers, isn't it?' she said politely. 'I believe we met in Tibet.'

Travers sat down rather shakily. Anne stared at him. 'Do you mean these are the two you told me about? The ones with the Doctor all those years ago?'

Travers nodded. Jamie peered into his face. 'Och aye, it's Mr Travers right enough. He's got awful old though,' he added tactlessly.

Slowly Travers said, 'When I met the Doctor in Tibet, he told me he'd already visited the Monastery— three hundred years before. He implied he could travel through Time.'

'Well, of course he can,' Jamie said impatiently. 'The thing is, do you know where he is now? We lost him in those tunnels.'

Anne shook her head. 'All I know is some soldiers were sent to look for him.'

Travers jumped to his feet. 'But this is wonderful! The Doctor's the one man who can help us. Come on, Jamie, let's see if they've found him.'

Travers bustled Jamie out of the room. Anne and Victoria turned to each other, both feeling rather abandoned. 'I'm still a bit puzzled about how you got here,' Anne said slowly.

Victoria sighed, 'Oh dear, I'm afraid it's all *very* complicated... You see, the Doctor has this machine called the TARDIS...'

In the Operations Room Travers found Sergeant Arnold, just returned from his fruitless search. 'Did you find the Doctor?' he demanded.

'Not a sign of him, sir. And he wasn't killed by the explosion because there was no explosion.' Briefly Arnold explained what they'd found on the platform. 'Somebody must have interfered with the charge.

Probably this mysterious Doctor.'

'Nonsense,' said Travers stoutly. 'The Doctor is an old friend of mine. He's—a scientific colleague. It's vital that we find him.'

Arnold looked sceptical. 'Well, whoever he is, he's vanished.'

'Maybe the Yeti got him,' said Jamie gloomily.

'If he isn't on their side.' Clearly Arnold hadn't abandoned his suspicions. He turned to Jamie. 'Look here, lad, if you want him found you'll have to help us. Any idea where he's gone?'

Jamie looked doubtfully at him. Although their coats were khaki rather than red, Jamie found it hard to forget that English soldiers were his traditional enemies.

'Now, lad, out with it,' Arnold said cheerily. 'Got some idea where he might be, have you?'

Jamie considered. It was at least possible that the Doctor would go to their arranged rendezvous. That or back to the TARDIS.

'Well?' persisted Arnold.

'I might have,' Jamie answered grudgingly.

'Then you'd better take me there—hadn't you?'

Jamie looked at Travers, who nodded. 'Better do as he says, Jamie. The sooner the Doctor's found, the better for all of us.'

Captain Knight and his men were fighting a rearguard action in the tunnels. They'd made their way down the Northern Line to Tottenham Court Road, then along the Central as far as Holborn. Outside Holborn

49

Station they had discovered the wrecked ammunition lorry and the bodies of the soldiers who'd been guarding it. The Yeti were nowhere in sight. Cases and boxes of explosives and ammunition were scattered everywhere.

Working as quickly as possible, Knight had ordered his men to gather up as much of the precious cargo as they could carry. Heavily laden they were making their way back through the tunnels. They had almost reached the Goodge Street Fortress when the Yeti attacked.

While the rearguard of his party fought desperately to hold off the Yeti, Captain Knight supervised the construction of a barricade of explosive-boxes across the tunnel where they'd been attacked. 'Right, that'll have to do,' he ordered. Standing up he cupped his hands and yelled, 'Corporal Lane—fall back!'

Lane and the other men were already in retreat, driven by the inexorable advance of the attacking Yeti. Roaring savagely the creatures stalked forwards, ignoring the bullets of the soldiers. His rifle empty, one of the soldiers reversed it and swung it like a club. A Yeti brushed the blow aside and smashed the soldier to the ground. Lane and the rest turned and fled, scrambling over the barricade to shelter behind it. From there they hurled their remaining grenades. As the explosions roared in the confined space, the Yeti staggered back and seemed to pause, waiting.

Captain Knight crouched beside Corporal Lane. 'Well done, Corporal. How many of them?'

'Only two, sir, but we couldn't hold 'em. Couple of the lads copped it.'

Movement behind sent them both spinning round, guns at the ready. A familiar voice called, 'Don't shoot, sir, it's me.' The burly form of Sergeant Arnold appeared from the semi-darkness, Jamie behind him. He took in the situation at the barricade with one swift glance. 'Yeti attack, sir?'

'That's right, Sergeant. Two of 'em, back down the tunnels.'

'What about the Holborn detachment, sir?'

'All done for. We got the ammo, though—some of it. Had to leave the rest.'

Arnold nodded, looking down the tunnel. The two Yeti were lumbering slowly forward again.

'Pull back and let them come on,' Knight whispered fiercely. 'Half this barricade's made of high explosive boxes. When the Yeti reach the barricade, I'll fire into the boxes and blow the lot sky high. With any luck it'll bring the roof down on them.'

'Maybe down on us too, sir.'

'We'll have to risk that. Now start moving the men back. I want you as far away as possible before I fire.'

The small group of soldiers retreated back as the Yeti came steadily on. By the time the Yeti reached the barricade, Knight and the others were almost out of sight round a curve in the tunnel. The two Yeti pushed aside the undefended barricade with ease. Then they stopped again. 'Now's the time, sir,' whispered Lane. 'They're standing right over the ammo boxes.' He peered down the tunnel. 'They seem to be using some kind of gun,' he sounded puzzled. 'It's spraying that cobwebby stuff over the boxes.'

'I'm going to blow them sky-high, cobwebs and all,' Knight said grimly. 'Give me your machine-gun, Corporal. The rest of you get down.' As the soldiers dropped to the ground, Knight stepped round the curve of the tunnel. Steadying the gun, he fired a long raking burst, right into the ammunition crates, then threw himself to the ground. There was a muffled thump and a blinding flash. Knight looked up. The two Yeti, quite unharmed, were standing beside the shattered crates. There was no sign of any other damage.

Slowly the Yeti resumed their advance. Knight turned. 'It's no good,' he yelled. 'Run for it. We'll have to get back to the Fortress.'

To his surprise no one moved. 'Too late, sir,' Lane said hoarsely. 'Look!' He pointed in the other direction. To his horror Knight saw two more Yeti coming up behind them. They were surrounded.

Victoria wandered aimlessly round the Common Room, wondering what to do with herself. Jamie had rushed off with his usual impulsiveness, forgetting all about her. Anne Travers had been very kind, but now she'd disappeared to help her father with his work. Victoria decided to go and look for them. Perhaps they'd let her make tea or wash test-tubes or something. Anything would be better than waiting on her own.

She left the Common Room and found herself in a long corridor painted a depressing War Office green. A soldier passed by carrying a clipboard and Victoria stopped him. 'Can you tell me where to find Professor Travers's laboratory please—I'm one of his assistants.'

The soldier seemed unsurprised. 'Just down there, miss, it's on your right.'

Victoria walked along to the laboratory door. She opened it cautiously, fearing to disturb some vital experiment, and heard the voice of Anne Travers say, 'Did you ever *see* this TARDIS, Father?'

She peeped through the door to see father and daughter working side by side at an equipment-crowded bench. Travers grunted, 'No, not really. Caught a glimpse of it. Thing like a Police Box, perched up on a mountain ledge. Then I got distracted. Saw a Yeti, a real one, not one of these blasted robots. Went chasing after it—lost it though. When I came back the Doctor and his friends and the Police Box had all vanished.'

Anne nodded. 'It's odd though, isn't it? Last time you saw the robot Yeti the Doctor turned up, and now here he is again.'

Travers grunted once more, not really listening.

Anne developed her theory. 'Perhaps the Doctor is really at the back of all this trouble. Maybe *he's* the one who controls the Yeti!'

Victoria didn't wait to hear any more. She tiptoed away from the door as quietly as she'd come. There was only one thought in her mind. She must get away from the Fortress, find the Doctor and warn him that he was already under suspicion.

It was a pity Victoria didn't stay to hear the rest of the conversation. Travers, thoroughly exasperated, put down the control sphere he was working on. 'My dear Anne, you're talking the most absolute rubbish,' he growled. 'The Doctor risked his life and the lives of his friends to defeat the Yeti and save Det-sen Monastery. Do you think he'd have done that if he was in league with them?'

Reassured Anne smiled. 'No, I suppose not. I must be getting jumpy, suspecting everyone!'

Travers sighed. 'Small wonder in a place like this. I only wish the Doctor would turn up now. I could do with his help.'

Jamie too was wishing that the Doctor would reappear. Together with Captain Knight, Sergeant Arnold and the rest of the soldiers, he was trapped in a section of tunnel, Yeti on either side. But strangely the Yeti made no move to attack. Instead they waited, occasionally exchanging the weird electronic bleeping sounds that served them as signals.

'This is getting on my nerves,' muttered Corporal Lane. 'Why don't they do something?'

Sergeant Arnold was imperturbable as ever. 'You just think yourself lucky, my lad. Good thing for us they *are* quiet.' He turned to Captain Knight. 'What about that explosion, sir? The explosives went off, but there was no blast.'

Knight said ruefully, 'Presumably that cobweb stuff absorbs the blast, dampens the whole thing down.'

'That'll be it, sir. Same thing must have happened at Charing Cross.'

'So I've blown up all our high explosive for nothing.'

Lane was still feeling the effect of the waiting. 'Can't we make a run for it, sir?' he appealed. 'Only two each end, we might get through.'

It was Jamie who answered. 'Och, dinna be so daft, man. We wouldna stand a chance, not while they're switched on.'

Knight glanced at him in surprise. 'And how do you know so much about it?'

Sergeant Arnold said, 'Seems he and this Doctor and the Professor are all old friends. They had trouble with these Yeti in Tibet years ago.' He turned to Jamie. 'That's right, isn't it, lad?'

'Aye, that's right enough,' said Jamie, hoping Knight wouldn't ask how many years ago. 'They're no' so frightening when you get used to them,' he added encouragingly.

Despite the dangerous situation, Knight couldn't help smiling at Jamie's casual manner. He looked at the grim forms of the Yeti as they stood on guard. 'If you know so much about them, maybe you can tell us how to deal with them?'

Jamie was quite willing to play the part of a Yeti expert. 'Well,' he began seriously, 'the thing to remember about these beasties is that they're no really beasties at all, they're a kind of robot. They're controlled by this sphere thing in their chest. Get hold of that and they're done for.'

'And how do you get close enough to do that without being killed?'

'Aye, well,' admitted Jamie reluctantly. 'That's the difficult bit!'

Suddenly Captain Knight interrupted him. 'Listen!' The signalling sound took on a higher note. At the same time, the two Yeti cutting off their retreat began to move slowly towards them. The trapped group of humans huddled against the tunnel wall, ready to face the final attack.

# 6

## The Terror of the Web

The Yeti on the far side showed no signs of movement. Only the second pair continued their steady advance. As they came closer the soldiers raised their guns for a final desperate resistance, though they knew that without grenades or explosives they were doomed... bullets alone had little effect on the Yeti. Suddenly Jamie whispered fiercely, 'Dinna fire. Just stand perfectly still.'

Knight looked at him in amazement. 'They're no making for us at all,' hissed Jamie. 'Look at the other two.' Sure enough the two Yeti that had first attacked them were moving away.

'Do as the boy says,' ordered Knight. The group stood still as the second pair of Yeti came up, passed them and followed the first pair down the tunnel. Soon all four Yeti had moved away out of sight.

Captain Knight let out a long sigh of relief. 'Now what the blazes made them do that?'

'I told you,' said Jamie. 'They're no natural beasties at all. They've been recalled. Now I wonder why...' He gazed after the departing Yeti in puzzlement.

'Never mind about why,' said Sergeant Arnold. 'Shouldn't we be getting back, sir?'

'Quite right, Sergeant. Don't want to push our luck.'

Baffled yet relieved, the small party set off towards the Fortress.

Private Weams came into the Operations Room, two mugs of steaming tea in his hand. He passed one to Corporal Blake. 'Here you are, Corp, brought you a nice cuppa...'

Blake reached out to take the tea then suddenly froze, his eyes fixed on the illuminated map. The light marking Euston Square was blinking steadily. 'The Web,' he gasped. 'It's started moving again!' He grabbed the internal phone. 'Get me Professor Travers!'

Seconds later Travers ran into the room, Anne and Chorley at his heels. Corporal Blake pointed to the map. 'Euston Square's gone already, Professor, *and* King's Cross. It's moved on to Farringdon.' Even as they looked, the Farringdon light flickered and went out.

Anne turned worriedly to her father. 'It's never moved as fast as this before...'

Blake's eyes were fixed on the board. 'Hasn't moved at all for two weeks, miss. Something's set it off again.'

Chorley had been sulking in his quarters when he heard the rumour of the new crisis. Now he seized the opportunity to push himself forward—and to get back at Travers. 'Isn't it strange, Professor, that this should happen on the very day your friend the Doctor turns up?'

'He *hasn't* turned up,' Anne pointed out. 'No one's seen him yet.'

'Ah, but what about those two young people? He could have sent them in here as spies.'

'Rot,' said Travers vigorously. 'I've already been through this nonsense with Anne. For the last time, the Doctor is a distinguished scientist and a personal friend. He's bound to turn up sooner or later. After all, his two young friends are here—and he certainly won't abandon them.'

'But they're not here,' said Chorley triumphantly. 'The young man's already gone off into the tunnels. Now the girl's vanished too.'

Anne looked at him in astonishment. 'Victoria's resting in the Common Room.'

'Not any more she isn't. I went to look for her a while ago—I wanted to ask her some more questions. She wasn't in the Common Room, and she's nowhere else in the Fortress either. I searched the whole place.'

'Why would she just go off like that?' Anne said worriedly.

'Because she was spying. Now she's gone back to this Doctor with her information.' Chorley was absolutely determined to build up Victoria's disappearance into a juicy spy scandal.

A shout from Weams interrupted them. 'Look at the board. The Web's moving again...' The Aldgate light began to flicker...

Corporal Blake looked at the clock. 'Time the Captain was back. Hope he's nowhere near that lot...'

Captain Knight and his men were on the last stages of their journey back to the Fortress. They were moving cautiously up to a junction when Knight heard a strange sound ahead. 'Listen!'

'Is it Yeti, sir?' whispered Arnold.

'Not unless they've learned to sing tenor,' replied Knight drily.

Now they could all hear it—a quavery tenor voice singing 'Men of Harlech', very much out of tune. A tall, spindly figure in army uniform was marching along the tunnel towards them. As he caught sight of them the singing trailed off. 'Hey, soldier!' yelled Arnold. The newcomer hurried towards them.

'Well, there's a sight for sore eyes, now,' he said in a broad Welsh accent.

Captain Knight looked at the skinny figure before him. The man had a round cheerful face with ears that stuck out like jug-handles. His uniform was crumpled and ill-fitting, his enormous boots badly needed a polish, and an oversize beret gave him the air of an elongated mushroom. Knight groaned out loud. 'Are you raving mad?' he whispered. 'Marching along these tunnels singing at the top of your voice?'

The man grinned disarmingly. 'Well, I was scared, see. I always sing when I'm scared.'

Sergeant Arnold had been watching the slovenly, unmilitary behaviour of the new arrival with mounting horror. Moving closer to him he muttered fiercely, 'Stand to attention when you're talking to an officer. Forgotten how to salute, have you? Name and number!'

The soldier crashed stiffly to attention, threw Knight a belated salute and bellowed, 'Six-O-One Evans, sir!' at the top of his voice.

'Sssh,' said Arnold in an agonised whisper.

'Six-O-One Evans,' the man whispered back.

Knight suppressed a smile. 'And what are you doing in these tunnels, Private Evans?'

'Trying to get out again, sir.'

'Don't be funny, lad,' said Arnold in a threatening whisper. 'Why are you down here in the first place?'

Evans lowered his voice dramatically. 'I was the driver, see, on that ammo truck to Holborn. We'd just unloaded when we got jumped by Yeti. I ran for it—then got lost.'

'Why didn't you get out the other way?'

'Couldn't, sarge. Tunnels are all blocked with this Web stuff. Moving towards me it was.'

Captain Knight spoke urgently. 'Moving? You're sure it was actually moving?'

'It was following a Yeti,' said Evans dramatically. 'Saw it myself. The Yeti came down the tunnel carrying a sort of glass thing, and the *Web* followed it...'

'This glass thing,' Jamie said urgently. 'Was it shaped like a pyramid?'

'That's right. A great glowing glass pyramid. How did you know?'

Jamie turned to Captain Knight. 'That pyramid is the home of the Intelligence. Smash it and you'll put the Yeti out of action.'

Before Knight could reply, Sergeant Arnold broke in, 'Excuse me, sir, but if the Web is on the move again, H.Q. could be in danger. Especially since we *didn't* manage to blow any tunnels.'

Knight nodded. The purpose of the demolition operations had been to create a safety zone around H.Q. by holding off the Yeti and the Web. 'Quite right, Staff. We'd better be moving.'

Jamie was outraged that no one had paid attention to his news. 'Och, you're not listening. Just smash yon pyramid and—'

'Don't argue with the officer,' growled Arnold. 'Get moving.'

Jamie felt suddenly obstinate. He'd had enough of trailing round meekly after soldiers. 'I will not. I came to find the Doctor, and I'm no' leaving till I have. And

I'll find that pyramid and smash it too, since you're too daft to listen!'

Arnold moved angrily towards him, but Knight intervened. 'All right, Sergeant, let him stay if he wants to. It's his own neck.'

Arnold moved reluctantly away. Unexpectedly Evans said, 'If the young gentleman's staying, I'd like to volunteer to help him, sir.'

Captain Knight considered. Evans, like Jamie, would be of little use in the Fortress, and if they were to be cut off every useless man would be a liability. 'Very well. Come along, Sergeant, move the men out. Good luck, both of you.'

As the soldiers started off, Jamie looked a little dubiously at his unexpected ally. 'Thanks for volunteering. It was verra brave of you.'

Evans grinned. 'Brave, me? Don't be daft, boyo. Just didn't fancy being trapped in that Fortress. First chance I get I'm skipping out of here.'

The group round the illuminated map watched worriedly as the Web continued its advance. 'There goes Liverpool Street,' said Weams. 'If this keeps up we could soon be completely surrounded. I reckon we should clear out while we can.'

Travers shook his head. 'No. The decision to evacuate can only come from Captain Knight.'

'Who happens to be still missing,' Anne Travers pointed out. 'Shouldn't you send a search party?'

Corporal Blake looked grim. 'We've got two parties out already, miss. We'll just have to sit tight and wait.'

'You can't abandon him.'

'I can't risk losing more men,' said Blake obstinately.

The argument ended when Captain Knight walked into the room. Anne ran to him. 'Are you all right?'

'More or less,' said Knight wearily. 'We lost quite a few men.'

Corporal Blake pointed to the map. 'Look at this, sir.'

Knight stared at the map in horror. 'When did all this start?'

'Soon after you left,' said Travers. 'Southern section is on the move too.'

'I gather there's a danger we may be cut off,' Chorley put in fussily. 'Captain Knight, don't you think you ought to evacuate?'

'If you want to leave, Mr Chorley, you're welcome to try.'

'What about the Doctor?' asked Travers.

'No sign of him. Once the Yeti attacked, we were too busy to look.' Knight explained what had happened on his expedition, telling them how Jamie had insisted on staying behind.

'So all three of them are out there,' said Anne Travers sadly. She told Knight of Victoria's disappearance.

Professor Travers tugged worriedly at his beard. 'I'm concerned about the young people, of course, but it's the Doctor I really want to see. I'm convinced he could help us.'

'Better not rely on the Doctor too much,' said Chorley spitefully. 'With the Yeti prowling those tunnels and the Web on the move again—the Doctor and his friends are probably dead by now.'

Jamie and his reluctant ally emerged from a tunnel and climbed on to the station platform. Evans looked at the station sign, crossed to the wall-map and peered at it in the dim emergency lighting. 'Here we are, Cannon Street.' He pointed triumphantly to their position. 'Well out of the danger zone.'

'You're supposed to be taking me back towards King's Cross where you saw that Yeti with the pyramid.'

'You don't seriously *want* to find a Yeti do you?'

'I want to find that pyramid and smash it,' said Jamie determinedly. 'Come on. We can go on the Circle Line. Monument next, then Tower Hill.'

Evans groaned.

Ignoring his protests, Jamie led him on into the next tunnel. After another long tramp they emerged on to Monument Station. They went along the platform then into the tunnel, heading towards Tower Hill. They'd only gone a short way when Jamie stopped. 'It's getting lighter!'

A pulsating glow was coming from the tunnel ahead of them. It grew brighter and brighter...

Evans grabbed Jamie's arm. 'It's the Web, moving towards us. Back, boyo.'

They turned and ran back towards Monument Station. As they came on to the platform, both stopped in horror. A dense swirling mass was rolling along the platform towards them. It looked like fog, thought Jamie, fog somehow become horribly solid. It glowed and pulsated with evil life.

'Can't go forward, can't go back,' panted Evans. 'We're trapped!'

## 7

## Escape from the Web

The glowing, pulsating mass of the Web rolled towards them in terrifying slow motion. Suddenly they heard a high-pitched electronic shriek. From out of the Web stalked a Yeti, holding a small, glowing pyramid. As the Yeti moved, the Web rolled after it, like a well-trained and obedient monster.

Jamie and Evans turned to run, but the glow from the tunnel they had left was even brighter. Jamie looked round desperately for some escape, but could see none. They were hopelessly trapped, caught between two advancing masses of the Web. Suddenly Jamie noticed the rifle still slung over Evans's shoulder. He grabbed it, and thrust it into the man's hands. 'The pyramid!' he yelled. 'Shoot at the pyramid!'

'I'll try, boyo—but I'm a terrible shot!'

Evans put the rifle to his shoulder and fired. Nothing happened. The Yeti marched steadily nearer, the Web rolling behind it like a great wave. Evans fired again. Still nothing.

'Take it steady, man,' shouted Jamie. 'It's point-blank range now. You *can't* miss!'

With the Yeti only yards away, Evans squinted in concentration and fired his third shot. The glass pyramid exploded into gleaming fragments. The Yeti stopped, quite still. The electronic howl died away. The Web stopped too, its glow slowly fading.

Jamie looked at the frozen Yeti and gave a great gasp of relief. Then from behind him he heard the sound of another electronic signal, growing steadily louder. He whirled round. The light from the tunnel was still pulsating. It was getting brighter and closer... Jamie suddenly realised that the pyramid they'd destroyed must have contained only a fraction of the Intelligence's power, just enough to control that one Yeti. He became aware that Evans was tugging at his arm. 'Don't stand there mooning, boyo. Let's get out while we can!' They ran through the platform arch, the light of the approaching Web steadily brighter behind them.

Victoria was tired, lost and afraid. She had long regretted her attempt to warn the Doctor, realising that she had no hope of finding him in the endless maze of Underground tunnels. She had decided to go back to the Fortress and try to convince Anne Travers of the Doctor's innocence. Surely her father would speak up for him. Unfortunately by the time she had taken this decision she was already lost, and it had taken her what seemed hours to find the tunnel leading back to the Underground entrance of the Fortress. But she found her way to Goodge Street station at last, and began walking along the track to the branch tunnel which held the door to the Fortress.

Victoria was about to turn into the tunnel when she heard footsteps. Quickly she ducked into an alcove and crouched down. Making herself as small as possible she peeped out. Two pairs of boots came into view, the first highly polished, the second old and scuffed. Around them flapped rather baggy checked trousers. With a squeal of joy Victoria flung herself from the alcove and into the Doctor's arms. He said delightedly, 'Victoria, my dear girl, where have you been? And where's Jamie?'

'He came out to look for you.'

'Out of where?'

Victoria realised the Doctor knew nothing of their adventures since they'd parted. She gave him a rapid and confused account of Goodge Street Fortress. 'It's full of soldiers and radios and machinery. Professor Travers is there too—the man we met in Tibet only he's *years* older... and he's a Professor now...'

'I'm sorry to interrupt this rapturous reunion...' They turned to see Lethbridge-Stewart looking at them quizzically. 'I should like the answers to one or two questions. Who is this young lady?'

'Dear me,' said the Doctor, 'I seem to be forgetting my manners. Victoria, this is Colonel Lethbridge-Stewart. Colonel, this is Victoria.'

For the first time Victoria noticed the revolver in Lethbridge-Stewart's hand. 'What's he pointing that thing at us for?'

'I'm afraid the Colonel's still a little suspicious of me,' the Doctor said sadly.

Suddenly Victoria remembered. 'So is Anne Travers—Professor Travers's daughter. She thinks *you're* controlling the Yeti.'

'Oh, does she,' said Lethbridge-Stewart. 'The plot thickens, doesn't it? I think it's time I got you two back to the Fortress.'

'You know about this Fortress place, do you?' asked the Doctor.

'As a matter of fact, I do. I happen to be its Commanding Officer.'

The Colonel led them into the side-tunnel and some way along it. He stopped by a plain iron door, the same one through which Victoria had left, and pressed a hidden buzzer. The door opened and a suspicious sentry appeared. He was soon overawed by Lethbridge-Stewart, and led them inside. A few minutes later Victoria found herself back in the familiar surroundings of the Common Room. She and the Doctor began recounting their respective adventures, while Lethbridge-Stewart lounged against the wall, a picture of relaxed confidence.

Captain Knight hurried into the room and saluted smartly. Lethbridge-Stewart returned the salute. 'Captain Knight, I am Colonel Lethbridge-Stewart, taking over as your new C.O.'

Knight's manner was a little strained. It wasn't easy to question the credentials of a senior officer. 'Forgive me, sir, but we've received no formal notice of your arrival. We were expecting a new C.O. of course but...'

'You don't know me from Adam? Quite right, old chap. I'm glad you don't take things on face value.' He produced a sheaf of papers and handed them over.

Knight checked them carefully. 'Everything's in order, sir. Welcome to the Fortress. I'm sorry you find us in such a bad state. How did you get down here, sir?'

Lethbridge-Stewart chuckled. 'By a very roundabout route! I set off with the ammunition truck. Then we got ambushed. I was driven into a side tunnel, and got lost.'

'Evans didn't mention any other survivors,' said Knight.

'Evans?'

'Driver of the truck. He got away too.'

'Well, it was all pretty confused. Anyway, I wandered around for a while, and then ran into this Doctor chap.'

Preoccupied with the Colonel, Knight had scarcely noticed the meek figure seated next to Victoria. The

Doctor stood up. 'I wondered when you were going to get around to me.'

Professor Travers rushed into the room, hair and beard bristling with excitement. 'Doctor! My dear fellow, you've turned up at last. You don't know how glad I am to see you.'

They shook hands warmly. The Doctor, used to the changes wrought by time, had no difficulty in recognising his old friend. 'My word, old chap, it *has* been a long time, hasn't it?'

The clipped voice of Lethbridge-Stewart interrupted them. 'I gather you know this man, Professor Travers?'

Travers said impatiently, 'Should have thought that was pretty obvious. Don't know you, though!'

'I'm Colonel Lethbridge-Stewart, the new Commanding Officer.'

Travers was unimpressed. 'Are you now? Well, the Doctor is an old and valued colleague of mine. His arrival gives us our first real chance of solving this problem.'

'And the girl?'

'Victoria is my assistant,' the Doctor explained hurriedly.

'Come along, Doctor,' said Travers impatiently. 'We've got a lot of work to do. The Web's closing in, you know, time's running short. I'll take you straight to my lab. You come too, Victoria...' Still talking, he bustled the Doctor and Victoria away.

'I gather you give Professor Travers his head,' Lethbridge-Stewart remarked drily.

Knight grinned. 'Not much alternative, sir. He's a pretty strong-willed old boy. Besides, he is in charge on the scientific side. He's got the most important job to do, so I just let him get on with it.'

'*We've* got a job to do as well,' said Lethbridge-Stewart crisply. 'These scientist chaps can't work unless we protect them. I shall hold a formal briefing meeting later on, but right now I'd like you to put me in the picture. Just tell me everything that's been going on.'

While Captain Knight was recounting the long story of his attempts to deal with the Yeti and the Web, the Doctor was hearing an account of things from Travers. 'It's the Intelligence right enough,' Travers concluded gloomily.

'Not me?' asked the Doctor mildly.

Travers gaped at him 'Eh? What d'you mean?'

The Doctor nodded towards Anne. 'I gather this young lady had one or two suspicions.'

Anne looked shamefaced, and Travers grunted. 'Just idle chat, Doctor. I soon put her right, didn't I, Anne?'

She nodded. Now she had actually met the Doctor, it did seem impossible to associate this mild and gentle figure with anything as evil as the Intelligence. Unfortunately it seemed almost equally hard to see him as the brilliant scientist described by her father.

The Doctor smiled at her and said, 'I agree with Professor Travers, we're certainly dealing with our old enemy from Tibet. And I'll tell you something else. My guess is that the Intelligence was directly responsible for bringing *me* here!'

'Why should it do that?' asked Anne.

'Revenge perhaps. It's extremely *conceited*, and it must have hated defeat—or perhaps it has some other motive, one we don't know about yet.'

Travers seemed worried. 'Thank goodness you managed to give it the slip, Doctor. The terrible thing is, I feel it's all my fault.' He gestured towards a bench full of Yeti souvenirs—damaged control spheres, parts of broken Yeti, even some of the tiny Yeti models the Intelligence used as controls. 'I brought all this stuff back from Tibet with me. The monks were glad to see the back of it. There was one undamaged Yeti complete with control sphere. I needed money, so I sold the Yeti to the Julius museum. I kept the control sphere for myself. I was determined to find out how it worked. Fiddled with it for years on and off... Just as I seemed to be succeeding it disappeared.'

'Back to the Yeti in the museum,' said the Doctor. 'Once the sphere started working, the Intelligence was able to home in on it, and get to work again.'

Travers nodded. 'The Yeti in the museum provided it with a ready-made pair of hands.'

'I imagine it will also have found a *human* agent by now,' said the Doctor. 'That was the way it worked in Tibet. Some poor soul, outwardly normal, but in reality completely controlled by the Intelligence.'

While they were considering this uncomfortable thought, Captain Knight came into the room. He looked round at the silent group and spoke with mock severity. 'Look alive, you dozy lot! The new C.O. wants you all to attend a briefing meeting.'

Anne smiled, taking up the joke. 'We're not in the army yet, you know.'

Knight grinned. 'You'd better tell the Colonel. Kick-off in the Common Room in a few minutes, O.K.?'

As he turned to leave Victoria asked, 'I don't suppose there's any news of Jamie?'

Knight shook his head, his face grave. 'No,' he said gently. 'I'm afraid there's not. He's still missing.'

Jamie and Evans were resting on Tottenham Court Road Station. Evans groped in his pockets. 'Haven't got any small change, have you, boyo? I could fancy a bar of chocolate.'

Jamie shook his head. Evans wandered to a nearby chocolate machine and gave the handle a hopeful tug. To his astonishment the drawer opened, revealing a bar of chocolate. 'Well, there's lovely,' he said delightedly. He snapped the bar in two and gave half to Jamie. 'Come on, let's be moving.'

'You're in a hurry all of a sudden.'

Evans was looking at the map. 'Been thinking I have. With any luck these Yeti are like lightning. Won't strike twice in the same place. We're pretty close to Holborn here. That's where I get off. If I can only get back to my lorry, I'll be away like lightning myself.'

'You're not coming back to H.Q. then?'

'Don't need me, do they? I'd only be a hindrance. Anyway I'm a driver, see. Not supposed to get involved in all this dangerous stuff.'

'Och, all that interests you is saving your own skin,' said Jamie scornfully.

Evans grinned. 'Well, it's the only one I got,' he explained reasonably. 'Look, boyo, they don't stand a chance back in that Fortress. You hop it with me while you can.'

Jamie shook his head. '*I'm* not running out on my friends.'

Evans stood up. 'Well, I'm sorry to leave you, boyo, but you got to take care of number one in this world.' With a cheery wave he jumped back on to the line and disappeared down the tunnel to Holborn.

Jamie finished his chocolate and went to study the map. If he could find his way on to the Northern Line, the next station would be Goodge Street. If only the Web hadn't blocked the tunnels... Jamie went through the station arch, and followed the signs to the Northern

Line. The empty station was gloomy and cavernous in the dim emergency lighting and his footsteps echoed with a sinister hollowness. Jamie was in a fine state of nerves by the time he found the right platform and jumped down on to the track. He walked along the tunnels for some time, listening to the sound of his own footsteps. Then he stopped. Each footstep had an echo. Someone was following him along the tunnel. He stopped again. The footsteps stopped too. He moved on, and the ghostly footsteps followed him.

Jamie put on a spurt, ducked into an alcove and waited. After a moment's hesitation the footsteps started again, moving closer. To his astonishment, Jamie saw Evans creeping along the tunnel. Jamie stepped out of hiding and shouted, 'Boo!'

Evans jumped. He gasped with relief. 'Gave me a nasty fright you did, boyo.'

'I thought you were going to Holborn?'

'Well, I changed my mind see. Started thinking about what you said, about deserting my mates.'

Jamie gave him a sceptical look.

Evans said, 'Oh, all right then. I tried to get out but the gates were locked. I got scared on my own and came to look for you!'

Jamie looked at him in exasperation. Then he found himself smiling. There was something rather disarming about Evans's frank timidity. 'Och, come along, man.

Let's try to get back to the Fortress. Maybe the Doctor's turned up by now.'

The Doctor sat patiently in the Common Room while Colonel Lethbridge-Stewart lectured them all on the crisis. The Doctor had already picked up most of the information from Travers, but it was interesting to see it all set out in order.

Lethbridge-Stewart was very thorough. Using a slide projector as a visual aid he took them through the entire history of events, starting with the disappearance of Travers's reactivated sphere, followed by the vanishing of the Yeti in the museum. He covered the first appearances of the mist, followed by the appearance of the Web in the tunnels and finally the arrival of the Yeti. He described the Government's counter-measures, the setting up of a scientific investigation unit headed by Travers, here in the old war-time Fortress at Goodge Street, with a military unit to protect it. 'Unfortunately the enemy has counter-attacked in force. The Web has been moving steadily closer despite all our attempts to stop it.' He pointed to a wall map. 'Above ground, it covers roughly the area enclosed by the Circle Line. Underground, much of that same area is now invaded by the Web. We are besieged.' The Colonel tucked his cane back under his arm. 'So much for the past. Now let's have some constructive suggestions. Professor Travers?'

Travers obviously didn't care for the Colonel's military manner. He muttered rather sulkily, 'I've been working on a method of jamming the Yeti transmissions. My daughter is trying to develop a control unit to switch them off. So far we've not had much success. Now the Doctor's here I hope we'll do better.'

The Doctor smiled modestly, but said nothing. Lethbridge-Stewart passed on, 'Captain Knight?'

'We've not had much success either, sir. Communications are our main problem. The mist and the Web absorb radio waves a lot of the time, particularly over any distance. The Yeti cut phone lines as soon as they're laid. We've tried blowing tunnels to hold back the Web but they've managed to sabotage that too. We're running low on supplies and explosives, particularly hand-grenades. Whenever a truck tries to get through, the Yeti ambush it. They seem to know what we're planning to do before we start.'

As he finished his tale of woe, Knight seemed unaware of the implications of his words, but they were not lost on the Doctor. He looked round the faces in the room. Travers and his daughter, Harold Chorley, Colonel Lethbridge-Stewart and Captain Knight, Sergeant Arnold standing rigidly to attention. Had the Intelligence already chosen its agent? It could be anyone in the room—except of course for himself and Victoria.

Chorley jumped to his feet. 'Isn't it time we started discussing evacuation plans, Colonel? With the Web creeping steadily closer it will soon be too late.'

'There will be *no* evacuation. This Unit will remain at its post and attempt to defeat the enemy until the last possible moment.'

'Then you'll all die down here!'

'Sit down, Mr Chorley!' The whiplash of authority in the Colonel's voice slammed Chorley back in his seat.

Weams hurried into the room with a sheet of paper. 'Latest plottings of the Web movements, sir.'

The Colonel studied the report, his face grave. 'Queensway, Lancaster Gate, Strand, Chancery Lane, all gone in the last half-hour.' He moved to the map on the wall. 'How long do you think we've got, Professor?'

Travers studied the map. 'Difficult to say. At this rate, we're dealing in hours rather than days.'

'We need time,' said the Doctor. 'Time for Travers and myself to find the solution. If you can blow this tunnel here,' he pointed to the map, 'we can seal ourselves off for a bit.'

Lethbridge-Stewart nodded approvingly. 'Good practical suggestion. Explosives, Captain Knight?'

'Just about enough left for the job, sir.'

'Excuse me, sir,' said Sergeant Arnold. 'Suppose the Yeti smother the charge like they did last time?'

The Doctor looked thoughtful. 'Have you got anything on wheels? Something that will actually run along the track?'

Knight looked at Arnold, who said, 'I think there's a baggage trolley in stores somewhere. We could adjust the wheel-gauge...'

'Then it's simple. Load the explosives on the trolley and attach a timing device. Blow the thing up while it's still on the move—before the Yeti can use their Web-gun.'

'Excellent idea,' agreed the Colonel even more enthusiastically.

'Splendid,' said the Doctor. 'Captain Knight, if you and the Sergeant will see to the trolley, the Professor and I will rig up a detonator for you.'

Somehow the Doctor seemed to have taken charge.

There was a general bustle of movement as everyone started to go out. 'What about me?' said Chorley plaintively.

'Like to help, would you?' said the Colonel heartily. 'Splendid, you can be liaison officer, keep track of all our progress. Corporal Blake, see Mr Chorley has everything he needs. I think I'll just take a general look around, get my bearings... Let me know when things are organised.'

He hurried out of the room. Private Weams glanced at Captain Knight. 'Things seem to be moving a bit, sir. Think the Doctor's idea will work?'

Knight glanced at the map, thinking of the relentless advance of the Web. 'It had better...' he said grimly. 'Come on, let's get to the stores.'

The soldiers left, Victoria and Anne following the Doctor and Travers. Chorley was alone, staring at the map. An expression of cold calculation slowly spread over his face...

A short time later, the Fortress was humming with activity. Blake and Weams were in the Operations Room, plotting the movements of the Web. Travers, Anne and the Doctor, watched by Victoria, were happily rigging up a Yeti-proof detonator and timing device. A party of soldiers was wrestling with a heavy baggage trolley. In the midst of all this activity *someone* moved quietly along the outer corridor and opened the locking clamps on the door that led to the tunnels. The Fortress was open to attack.

# 8

## Return of the Yeti

Victoria put down the little Yeti with a shudder. The last time she'd seen such a model it had been in the hands of the old monk, Padmasambvha. Controlled by the great Intelligence, he was using the model to summon the Yeti for their attack on Det-Sen Monastery. The Doctor glanced up from his work. 'My word, that looks familiar. Doesn't work, does it?'

Anne Travers shook her head. 'It's dead, so are the others, all four of them.'

Victoria looked at the bench. 'Four? There's only one here.'

Travers spoke abstractedly. 'Others must be about somewhere. Have a look, will you?'

The Doctor and Travers returned to their work, while Victoria started hunting through the jumble of electronic parts and Yeti relics on the bench. But she didn't find the missing model Yeti. Unseen hands had already placed *one* of them in a dark corner just outside the Explosives Store. The Yeti model was giving out a faint, almost inaudible, electronic bleep.

In the tunnel near the Fortress, a Yeti stood motionless, waiting. As the signal from the model reached it, it jerked into life and began lumbering slowly towards the Fortress.


Professor Travers made a few last-minute adjustments to his detonator. 'There you are, Doctor, that what you wanted?'

'Splendid, old chap. I'll just wire it into my timing mechanism...'

The Doctor began attaching Travers's detonator to an intricate device of his own construction. Suddenly he noticed that Victoria was on the point of tears. 'What on earth is the matter, my dear?'

'Don't you see, Doctor? You've forgotten all about Jamie. If this plan of yours works, he'll be cut off from us too!'

The Doctor stopped and put his arm round her shoulders. 'I haven't forgotten Jamie, my dear, not for one moment. But I have to think of the lives of every single person in this Fortress. And we can't defeat the Intelligence *or* help Jamie, unless we manage to survive ourselves.' Patting her on the back, the Doctor returned to his work.

*

The Fortress door slid smoothly open, revealing the towering figure of a Yeti. It held a Web-gun in its giant hands. The Yeti paused for a moment, then swung round as it picked up a signal. Moving with astonishing quietness, it progressed along the corridor to a door marked 'DANGER—HIGH EXPLOSIVES'. An enormous metal padlock secured the door. The Yeti reached out a huge claw and twisted off the padlock as if it was made of plasticine. It tossed the padlock into the corner beside the model Yeti, then lumbered into the Explosive Store.

In the Operations Room, the Doctor was showing the linked device to Colonel Lethbridge-Stewart. 'This is set to explode sixty seconds after you switch it on. You can vary the timing with this control here. If you roll the trolley from the top of a gradient you should have ample time to get clear.'

'Suppose the Yeti get to it first?'

'If anyone interferes with the device, it will switch off immediately,' said the Doctor with simple pride. Lethbridge-Stewart nodded approvingly. Funny little chap, this Doctor, but he certainly knew what he was about.

Sergeant Arnold hurried in. 'I think we're in trouble, sir. When we went to take the trolley out—we found the main door open.'

'Why wasn't it guarded?' snapped the Colonel.

Captain Knight had followed the sergeant into the room. 'I'm afraid there was a mix-up, sir. The sentry was detailed to the trolley party. Sergeant Arnold thought I'd replaced him, I thought he had. Entirely my fault, sir.'

'Beg your pardon, sir, it was mine,' volunteered Arnold. 'I must have misunderstood the order.'

'We'll work out the blame later,' the Colonel said grimly. 'I want to know what's going on here.'

'I'm afraid there's worse to come, sir,' said Knight. 'One of the men found this on the floor outside the Explosives Store. *This* was beside it.' Knight held out the twisted remains of a heavy padlock—and one of the missing Yeti models. He put them on a nearby table.

The Doctor said, 'Has anyone been in the Explosives Store since this happened?'

Knight shook his head. 'I put a guard on the door and came to report straight away.'

Lethbridge-Stewart was already on his way, and Knight and the Doctor followed. Weams picked up the model Yeti from the table and examined it curiously.

Two soldiers stood nervously in the corridor, guns levelled at the door of the Explosives Store, as Lethbridge-Stewart and his group came to a halt and listened. Everything was quiet.

'You think there's someone in there, Doctor?' whispered Knight.

'Someone or something,' answered the Doctor grimly. 'And there's only one way to find out.' Before anyone could stop him the Doctor stepped forward and flung open the door, revealing a sight that froze them with horror. The entire storeroom was packed with the pulsating, glowing mass of the Web. The Doctor slammed the door shut and stepped back. 'Well,' he said mildly. 'Now we know! I'd get that door solidly barred if I were you.'

Knight looked at Arnold, who grabbed the nearest soldier and began issuing a stream of orders. Knight, Lethbridge-Stewart and the Doctor walked back to the Operations Room. The Colonel was deep in thought. 'Holborn!' he said suddenly. 'Captain Knight, remember how you went to recover the ammunition from the Holborn supply truck?'

'We had to blow that up, sir, when we were attacked.'

'But you weren't carrying *all* the ammunition, were you? Some had to be left at Holborn. It may still be there.'

'Perhaps so,' agreed the Doctor dubiously. 'But since the Yeti have dealt with the explosives here, they've probably done the same with the rest of the Holborn stuff.'

'Still it's a chance,' insisted the Colonel. 'And it seems to be the only one we have.'

The Doctor knew it was no use trying to argue. Lethbridge-Stewart was the kind of soldier who didn't know the meaning of surrender. If the worst came to the worst he'd die fighting the enemy with his bare hands.

Sergeant Arnold came in and saluted. 'Search completed, sir. No sign of Yeti inside the Fortress.'

'Excellent. Get a squad ready to leave for Holborn right away.'

'Sir!' Arnold saluted again and left the room.

Lethbridge-Stewart turned to Captain Knight. 'Better tell the Professor what we're doing.'

'What about our liaison officer, Mr Chorley?'

'Less anyone tells him the better. Only gave him the job to keep him quiet. I'll leave some men behind, Doctor. You and the Professor will be quite safe here.'

'Will we? Don't forget, Colonel, someone here is under the control of the Intelligence. That door didn't open itself—and someone had to place this model to guide the Yeti.'

'Traitor in the camp, eh? Then we must find him!'

'How can we? We were moving about all over the place when it happened. Could have been anyone—even you, Colonel!'

'Or you, Doctor?' They looked at each other for a moment, and then the Colonel smiled. 'We've got to trust someone, Doctor, so we may as well start with each other. I'll keep an eye on my party, you take care of things here, eh?'

The Doctor nodded, curiously pleased by the Colonel's trust. Starchy sort of fellow this Colonel, but a man you could rely on. Unaware that this was the beginning of a long friendship, they both hurried out of the room.

In the Common Room, Victoria was chatting to Harold Chorley. She'd gone to make some tea and found him sitting in lonely state, a liaison officer no one wanted to liaise with. He seemed grateful for her company, and was being exceptionally charming. Chorley was a skilled interviewer, who knew how to use the soft approach when it paid him. To her surprise, Victoria was soon telling him all about the TARDIS. Chorley listened, struggling to understand. 'And you say this machine of the Doctor's could get you out of here?'

'Yes, of course it could. The TARDIS can go anywhere.'

'And it's still at Covent Garden where you left it?'

'I suppose it must be.'

'Then why doesn't the Doctor use it to rescue us all?'

'I suppose he will, if there's no alternative. But he won't leave until Jamie turns up. And now they're going to blow up the tunnel...' Victoria held back a sob.

The Doctor came into the room and looked at them, sensing something strange in the atmosphere.

Chorley spoke in a strained voice. 'We were just talking about you, Doctor... I hadn't realised...' Suddenly he rushed from the room.

The Doctor looked after him in astonishment. 'What's the matter with him?'

'I think he's worried about them blowing up the tunnel.'

'He needn't be—I doubt if they'll succeed,' said the Doctor. 'Anyway, why should he worry about that?'

'He's got some idea you could take us all away in the TARDIS—he doesn't want us to be cut off from it.'

'Victoria—you didn't tell him about the TARDIS?'

Victoria nodded. It was impossible to explain the impact of Chorley's charm. 'You don't think he wants to steal it?' she asked in sudden alarm.

'I wouldn't put it past him.' The Doctor tried the door. It was locked. 'Oh, Victoria,' he said reproachfully. Victoria started to cry.

As Harold Chorley hurried to the Fortress exit, he was surprised to find it open. Jamie and Evans, back at last, were just being admitted by a suspicious sentry. 'Has the Colonel's party already left?' Chorley gasped breathlessly.

It was Jamie who answered. 'Aye, they're already off to Holborn. We passed them on the way down the tunnel.'

Before anyone could stop him, Chorley dashed into the tunnel. The sentry decided he could look after himself, and closed and barred the door again. Jamie and Evans moved along the Fortress corridors. They heard a muffled banging from the door of the

Common Room, which seemed to be locked on the outside. Jamie unlocked and opened the door. Victoria and the Doctor fell out almost on top of him. There was a brief and rapturous reunion which the Doctor interrupted by saying urgently, 'Jamie, have you seen Chorley?'

'Aye, just a minute ago. He went out as we came in. Seemed in a rare old state, too.'

'Come on!' The Doctor ran down the corridor. Jamie and Victoria looked helplessly at each other and set off in pursuit. After a moment's hesitation, Evans followed *them*. There was clearly something nasty going on here, and he didn't want to face it alone. Maybe there would be safety in numbers.

He caught up with them just as the Doctor was persuading the reluctant sentries to open the main door yet again.

'What do you think I am,' one of them grumbled. 'Doorman at Harrods?'

Jamie, the Doctor, Victoria and Evans rushed out into the tunnels. The sentry slammed the door behind them and turned back to his mate. 'This time it stays closed.'

A giant shape began moving quietly down the corridor towards them.

Travers threw down his tweezers in disgust, and looked up from the control sphere. 'Well, where *is* the Doctor, then? I've gone as far on this as I can without his help. Gives you a job to do and then disappears.'

Anne smiled. 'Shall I go and see if he's back yet?'

Before Travers could reply, there was a distant thump, and a muffled scream. Travers got to his feet. 'Stay here, Anne.' Ignoring her protests, he moved into the corridor.

Everything seemed quiet. Travers began moving towards the direction of the sound. The noise appeared to come from the Operations Room. He walked along the corridor and looked inside.

Private Weams lay sprawled on the ground. Travers ran to him at once, and knelt by the body. Weams was quite dead, his neck broken by a single savage blow. On the floor beside him lay the model Yeti.

As Travers reached for it, a shadow fell over him. He looked up. Moving towards him was the massive form of a Yeti. Travers rose and backed away. The Yeti moved closer, reaching out for him...

# 9

# Kidnapped!

Travers's first thought was for his daughter. He backed towards the door, shouting as loudly as he could. 'Anne! The Yeti are here! Run and hide!'

The Yeti lunged.

In the laboratory, Anne Travers heard her father's voice. 'Anne... the Yeti... hide—' Suddenly the voice choked off. She ran towards the door—and into a Yeti. The Yeti's arm flashed out in a casual sweep that sent Anne flying across the room. She crashed into a bench, slid down and rolled underneath it. The Yeti looked at her crumpled motionless form. Methodically it began to wreck the laboratory. When the place was a shambles, it turned and lumbered away.

As it moved along the corridor, another Yeti appeared from the Common Room. It dragged the unconscious Travers behind it, as a child drags a teddy-bear by one arm. The two Yeti and their captive moved towards the exit. The door was standing open, the cobwebbed bodies of the sentries sprawled beside it.

The Yeti, with their prisoner, disappeared into the tunnels.

Jamie, the Doctor and Private Evans were racing along the tunnels in the direction of Covent Garden. Jamie tried to argue with the Doctor—never an easy thing to do, particularly when running at full speed.

'What does it matter if this Chorley does get to the TARDIS? He canna operate it. He won't even be able to get in.'

'Not if he's a normal human being, Jamie. But suppose he's been taken over? The last thing we want is the TARDIS in the hands of the Intelligence.'

'Aye, you're right there,' Jamie shuddered at the thought.

'We're nearly there,' said the Doctor encouragingly. 'If we go down this tunnel here—' He turned and stopped, pointing. 'Look!' A glowing, pulsating mass filled the tunnel before them. 'The Web has beaten us to it.'

Victoria tugged at the Doctor's sleeves. 'So we can't get to the TARDIS after all?'

'I'm afraid not, Victoria.'

Jamie looked at the glowing Web with distaste, remembering how it had nearly trapped him. 'What's happened to Chorley?'

'Just what I was thinking, Jamie. I wonder if he reached the TARDIS before the Web arrived.' The Doctor started walking towards the glowing mass.

Jamie tried to stop him. 'Doctor, don't be so daft!'

'It's all right, Jamie, it doesn't seem to be on the move. I just want a sample for analysis. Anyone got a container?'

Evans produced a worn and shiny tin. 'There's this—but I'm very attached to it.'

The Doctor took the tin from him, opened it and tipped out the contents; some rather dry tobacco and a packet of cigarette papers.

'Hey, that's my baccy,' protested Evans.

'Smoking's very bad for you,' the Doctor reproved. He walked up to the Web and fished a pair of tweezers from his pocket, using them to tease a fragment of the Web away from the main mass. Dropping the curious cotton-wool like substance into the tin, he handed it back to Evans. 'Here's your precious tin—*you* look after it!'

As if resenting the Doctor's attack, the Web began to glow and pulse with light, giving out its high electronic shriek. Slowly it started to billow towards them. 'You've set it off again now,' said Jamie.

The Doctor called out to his companions, 'Come on everybody, run for it.' They pelted off down the tunnel, leaving the angrily pulsating Web behind them.

Turning a corner they ran suddenly into a party of soldiers, who instinctively swung their rifles to cover them.

'All right, Sarge,' yelled Evans. 'Don't shoot, it's only us.'

Sergeant Arnold lowered his rifle. 'You'll pop up once too often some day, my lad.'

The Doctor, Jamie and Victoria caught up. 'Any luck with the explosives at Holborn?' asked the Doctor.

Arnold shook his head. 'The Web beat us to it. Blocked the tunnels just before we arrived.'

'Aye,' said Jamie, 'the same thing happened to us. Seems to know what we're planning every time. What are you lot doing here?'

'Waiting for the Colonel. He's taken a party on a recce to see if they can find a way through to Holborn by the Piccadilly Line. If they don't come back, we assume the way is open and follow. What are you doing?'

'Looking for Chorley,' explained the Doctor. 'He seems to have got himself lost.'

Arnold grunted. 'That won't break anyone's heart. I'd like you all to go back to H.Q. at once, please, Doctor. These tunnels are no place for civvies.' It was obvious from Arnold's tone that this was an order rather than a request.

The Doctor accepted the instruction meekly. 'I expect you're right. I've got work to do anyway—and I've taken a sample of the Web. I want to show it to Professor Travers.'

Arnold nodded dismissively. 'Off you go, Doctor. I'll tell the Colonel about you when I see him. Right, lads, time we were on our way.'

The soldiers moved off, and the Doctor and his little group hurried back towards H.Q. The rest of the journey was quiet enough. But when they reached the Fortress door it was open wide, light streaming into the dimly-lit tunnel. They went inside, stopping horrified at the sight of the cobwebbed bodies. The Doctor led them quickly past. 'Come on, we must find out what's happened.'

They looked into the empty Common Room, then continued along the corridor. As they approached Travers's laboratory they heard a faint moaning sound. They hurried inside and saw Anne Travers struggling to her feet. The Doctor ran to help her. She looked at him fearfully. 'The Yeti... have they gone?'

The Doctor nodded. 'No sign of them now.'

'My father... what's happened to him?'

The Doctor led her to a seat. 'Don't worry, we'll find him. Look after her, Victoria, will you? Better go to the Common Room and bathe that cut.'

The Doctor, Jamie and Evans searched the Fortress for Travers, but found no trace of him, living or dead. As they were making their way to the Common Room, Jamie said, 'What do you reckon happened to him, Doctor?'

'The Yeti must have taken him.'

'Why would they do that?' Evans demanded. 'Why not just kill him?'

'I don't know—unless they had a use for him...'

They heard the clatter of booted feet. Lethbridge-Stewart, Knight, Arnold and a party of soldiers came running along the corridor. The Doctor greeted them with relief. 'Glad to see you're all right. You didn't make it to Holborn then?'

The Colonel shook his head. 'The Web was blocking the tunnels. Doctor, what the devil's been happening here?'

'Yeti broke in when we were hunting Chorley. We think they've taken Professor Travers.'

'How did they get in?'

'Presumably someone helped them again.'

The Colonel shook his head, baffled. 'Once they were inside they could have destroyed the entire Fortress. Or laid an ambush for the rest of us.'

'They came for Travers. And they took him.'

'Why would they do that?'

The Doctor shrugged. 'Who knows? Perhaps they had a use for him.'

They were interrupted by Corporal Blake. 'I think you'd better come and see the indicator board, sir—'

The Doctor went with Lethbridge-Stewart to the Operations Room and stood looking at the map. One by one the station indicator lights were flickering and going out. Oxford Circus, Green Park, Trafalgar Square. There were only five lights still on the board—Piccadilly Circus, Leicester Square, Tottenham Court Road, Goodge Street and Warren

98

Street. 'This time the Web is really closing in,' said the Colonel grimly.

The Doctor nodded. 'We're the fly all right. But where's the spider?'

'Give the others a hand clearing up, will you, Corporal Blake?' said the Colonel. When Blake was gone he turned to the Doctor. 'This theory of yours— that someone amongst us is working with the Yeti. Could it have been Travers all along?'

'I doubt it. Why stage the attack? He could simply have gone off to join them. Now Chorley did just quietly disappear and I'd say he was a much more likely candidate. On the other hand, the person in league with the Intelligence could still be among us.'

'I am uncomfortably aware of that fact! Well, what now?'

'I must get on with Travers's work just as fast as I can.'

'Do you think you can succeed in time, Doctor?'

'To be honest I'm not sure,' the Doctor replied sadly. 'With the state the laboratory's in... Now if I could reach the TARDIS... I've got all kinds of equipment in there... But that's impossible.'

'Where is this TARDIS of yours?'

'Somewhere near Covent Garden.'

'And what does it look like?'

'Like a Police Box,' said the Doctor simply. 'But there's no chance of reaching it now. I have a feeling the Intelligence knows about it—and the Intelligence wants me trapped here. The TARDIS will be well guarded by now. I'll see what I can do in the laboratory. Anne will help. I expect I can bodge something up.'

When the Doctor had gone, Colonel Lethbridge-Stewart stood staring at the map. The enemy was closing in—and he was powerless to fight back. The deaths of his men at the Fortress had left him in a state of helpless anger. Now he was condemned to wait, while the Doctor 'bodged something up'. By the time Captain Knight came into the room, the Colonel had reached a decision. 'Pick me a squad of the fittest men and have them ready to move out. The Doctor has some important scientific equipment in a box near Covent Garden. I'm going to fetch it for him.'

The Doctor, Jamie, Victoria and Anne Travers were clearing up the mess in the laboratory. As they straightened the benches and tried to get the equipment back into some kind of order, Anne Travers said, 'But why did they take him, Doctor?'

The Doctor lifted a broken piece of equipment. 'Presumably because he was a danger to them. He was working on a way to deal with the Yeti, wasn't he, and fairly near to success?'

'We were almost ready to test a kind of control unit I'd built—that thing you're holding. Father was trying

100

to activate another sphere!' Anne produced it from her pocket. 'Luckily I was working on it myself when they attacked... I don't think it was damaged when I fell.'

The Doctor examined Anne's control unit. 'Oh yes, a splendid piece of work—and nearly complete. If we can repair this, and add a few improvements, it will certainly control the sphere. But will it actually over-ride commands transmitted by the Intelligence?'

'*Can* you repair it, Doctor?'

The Doctor looked at the piles of shattered equipment. 'I *can*—if we can find all the bits I need.'

Private Evans sidled into the room, shaking his head at the sight of the damage. 'Right old mess, innit? Sergeant Arnold said I'd better give you this, Doctor. It was found in the Ops Room, see?'

The Doctor said, 'You know what this is, don't you? A homing device to fetch the Yeti! And you're giving it to me!'

Hurriedly Evans handed the model over. The Doctor placed it carefully on a bench. 'I must get this dismantled. It's like walking around with a Time Bomb, having one of these.' He clamped it in a vice and unscrewed the base. 'That should fix it.'

Evans took a tin from his pocket. 'Here's your sample of that Web stuff, Doctor. I'd like the tin back when you've finished with it.' Handing over the tin, Evans backed hurriedly out of the room.

The Doctor ran his fingers through his hair. 'So many things to do at once! I'd better have a quick look at this stuff. Got a handling shield, Anne?'

Anne Travers looked in a locker and fished out a transparent box. Set into one side were a pair of heavy protective gloves on the end of little 'sleeves'. The Doctor put the tin in the box and closed it, then slipped his hands into the gloves.

Jamie looked on in astonishment. 'You're making a right old fuss, Doctor.'

'We're dealing with an unknown quantity, Jamie. Can't be too careful. Now stand back everybody.'

Fumbling a little in the heavy gloves, the Doctor opened the tobacco tin. As the lid came off, the others saw an expression of astonishment appear on his face. They crowded round to look. The tin was empty.

# 10

## Danger Above Ground

At the head of the stairs, leading to the upper exits, Colonel Lethbridge-Stewart was concluding his briefing. 'We'll open Goodge Street Station, and go out that way. Once on the surface, my party will approach Covent Garden from Neal Street. Sergeant Arnold, with Private Evans and Corporal Lane, will take the trolley through the tunnels and arrive at the same time as ourselves. One party should get through, hopefully both. We'll be looking for a blue Police Box. As soon as it's found, I want it either on the trolley or out of the station by the surface route, as quickly as possible. Captain Knight will stay here to look after the civilians. Everyone got grenades? Time to go!' The Colonel led his squad out of the surface door.

Meanwhile, in the tunnel outside the lower main door, Lane and Evans began shoving the trolley along. Evans was already groaning in protest. 'Shouldn't be doing this really, Sergeant. Driver, that's my job.'

'Don't you come the old soldier with me, lad,' roared Arnold. 'And don't try skiving off either. 'Cause if you do—I'll get you—understand? Now shove!'

Slowly the trolley trundled away down the tunnel.


Captain Knight looked at the Doctor in astonishment. 'Evans? You can't really suspect that he's working with the Intelligence. The man's such an idiot!'

'That would make it all the easier for him to be taken over,' the Doctor pointed out. 'First he brings me that Yeti model—now my Web sample disappears in his charge. I certainly think we ought to question him.'

'I'm afraid we can't. He's gone off with the others—to get your TARDIS back for you.'

'What did you say?' The Doctor listened appalled as Knight told him of Lethbridge-Stewart's departure. 'I warned him it was hopeless,' he burst out angrily. 'The TARDIS will be too well guarded.'

'He realised the danger, I'm sure,' Knight said quietly. 'But I think he felt he had to do something. It isn't easy you know—just waiting for you chaps to come up with the answer!'

The Doctor nodded, realising the dilemma of men trained for action who found themselves completely unable to act. 'This makes my next request all the more urgent, Captain Knight. Our only hope of defeating the Intelligence now lies in my completing Professor

104

Travers's work. The Yeti wrecked his laboratory, and I need a fresh supply of electronic spare parts.'

'According to the Colonel you've got all you need in this TARDIS thing. So if he brings it back for you...'

'He won't,' said the Doctor decisively. 'The best we can hope for is that he manages to get back alive. I must have those parts immediately, and I shall have to go to the surface to get them. Luckily this area is packed with electronic shops. It'll take me only a few minutes to find what I need.'

Knight considered. 'Very well, Doctor, but on one condition—I come with you!'

Sergeant Arnold, Private Evans and Corporal Lane brought their trolley to a creaking halt. Blocking the way was a solid wall of the Web, glowing with a faint, sinister light. Arnold was checking the fastening of a long coil of rope attached to the rear of the trolley. He looked up, satisfied, and took two respirator packs from inside the trolley. 'Right, here's the plan. Two of us put these on and go through the Web with the trolley to Covent Garden. Third man stays here on the rope. He pulls the trolley back once we get this box loaded, or *us* back if we get into trouble.' He looked at the two soldiers. 'Now, I want one volunteer to go through the Web with me and the trolley. We should be all right in the respirators.' No one moved. 'All right, I'll go alone.'

'That's an uphill gradient, Sarge,' said Lane. 'It'll take two of us to shift the trolley.' He reached out and took the other mask.

Evans looked at them in frank amazement. 'Potty, you are, both of you.'

'That's enough out of you,' said Arnold. 'Now, all you've got to do is feed us the rope as we go in, pull us back if there's any sign of trouble. Think you can manage that?'

Evans nodded. The two others put on their respirators and started moving the trolley into the Web. It parted like solid smoke, and soon they disappeared from sight. Evans paid out the rope as ordered, peering anxiously into the Web. Suddenly its glow began to increase in intensity and an earsplitting electronic wail filled the tunnels. Evans dropped the rope, clutching his ears in agony. From inside the Web came the sound of a muffled human scream... then silence.

Somewhere Evans found unexpected resources of courage. He stayed at his post, hauling desperately on the rope. The trolley slid smoothly back along the down gradient. As it emerged from the Web, Evans saw Corporal Lane spreadeagled across it. The gasmask had been wrenched from his face, which was covered with the thick, fluffy substance of the Web. He was quite dead. Of Sergeant Arnold, there was no trace.

Evans's nerve finally broke. Dropping the rope, he tore frantically down the tunnel.

Colonel Lethbridge-Stewart and his men were fighting for their lives. As soon as they'd reached the surface, Yeti had appeared to ambush them, tracking them through the misty streets, anticipating their every move. Now the soldiers had taken refuge in a warehouse yard, and still the Yeti were closing in from all sides. Many of them carried Web-guns. The Colonel threw a grenade, and saw a Yeti stagger back from the blast. He reached for another but the bag was empty. At his side, Corporal Blake yelled, 'I'm out too, sir, so are most of the lads.'

Lethbridge-Stewart realised that with the grenades gone their position was hopeless. No other weapons seemed even to delay the Yeti, let alone stop them. He stood up, cupping his hands, 'All right, men, scatter and run for it. Don't bunch up, take different directions. Now, go!'

The Colonel himself sprinted for the warehouse wall, running, dodging men all around. Some were smashed to the ground by Yeti, or smothered by the Web-guns, but others seemed to be getting through. The Colonel became aware of Blake close to him. 'Run clear, man,' he yelled. Two men together made an obvious target. But the warning was too late. Blake crumpled, choked by the stifling blast of a Web-gun. Dodging a slashing blow from a Yeti, Lethbridge-Stewart jumped for the top of the wall and swung himself over. He dropped to his feet in the street outside and began sprinting for the Goodge Street tube entrance. He was determined to get back to the Fortress, to see things through to the end.

The Doctor was busily engaged in looting a Goodge Street electronics shop. At the back of his mind he hoped that the Government would remember to pay compensation. The owner of the shop had been no believer in system, and all his spares were jumbled on the shelves, mostly in unlabelled boxes. Captain Knight stood on guard in the doorway. In the distance could be heard the dull thump of grenades. He looked out into the mist, wondering what was happening to the Colonel and his men. Over his shoulder he called, 'Haven't you done yet, Doctor?'

The Doctor scrabbled in a carton. 'Nearly. Just need one more component... I'll try in the back.'

The Doctor disappeared into the back store-room. Knight waited. He kept thinking he could hear the faint electronic sound of a Yeti signal. It seemed to be very close... Suddenly two enormous shaggy figures loomed out of the mist, eyes glowing red, fangs bared in a savage roar. The Yeti had found them.

The Doctor heard the roars just as he found his vital missing component. Stuffing it in the box with the others, he ran into the shop. Two Yeti waited there. The body of Knight lay sprawled in the shop doorway.

For what seemed a very long time, the Doctor and the two Yeti stood facing each other. Then the Yeti wheeled and moved away, out of the shop and into the mist.

The Doctor hurried across to Knight. He was dead, killed by a single slashing blow. Sadly the Doctor straightened up. Then he paused. Somehow he still seemed to hear a faint Yeti signal. It was coming from Knight. The Doctor searched the pockets of the dead man. Soon he felt a familiar shape. From out of Knight's pocket he took a model Yeti. Jumping to his feet the Doctor hurried from the shop.

He had reached the entrance of Goodge Street Station when he heard footsteps coming through the mist. A voice called, 'Doctor!' He turned to see Lethbridge-Stewart running towards him.

Private Evans was feeling distinctly aggrieved. Returning to the Fortress in the role of surviving hero, he was being sharply questioned by the Colonel, the Doctor and almost everyone else. 'Look,' he protested, 'it's no use trying to pin anything on me.' He glanced furtively round the crowded laboratory. The Colonel, the Doctor, Jamie, Victoria and Anne Travers looked suspiciously back. 'I didn't pinch your rotten Web sample. And I didn't plant no Yeti model on the Captain, neither.'

'You know,' said the Doctor, 'I'm inclined to believe you.' He held up a Yeti model. 'Here's the one you gave me. I put that out of action straight away. Here's the one I found on poor Captain Knight!' He put it in a vice, applying a vicious squeeze to the lever and crushing the Yeti's base. 'Now that one's harmless. But there were three Yeti models unaccounted for—and the third is still missing.'

Lethbridge-Stewart shook his head. 'It's like a nightmare. An enemy we can't see or touch, who knows our every move. Out there in the street, the Yeti were waiting for us every time. Wherever we went, whatever we did, it was still no good...' He stopped, aware that the Doctor was staring at him in horror. 'What is it, Doctor?'

'Don't you realise what you're saying?' the Doctor said sharply. 'Colonel—turn out your pockets. Quickly now!'

Dumbly, Lethbridge-Stewart obeyed. He produced keys, money, notebook, wallet—and the tiny model of a Yeti. It started bleeping faintly. 'That's why they tracked you so easily,' said the Doctor grimly.

He was reaching for the Yeti model to make it safe when the door smashed open. The vast, shaggy bulk of a Yeti filled the entrance.

With curious formality the Yeti entered the room and took a position to one side of the door. A second Yeti entered and stood on the other side. Then Professor

110

Travers came in. He stood like a barbaric monarch, flanked by guards.

'Father!' cried Anne joyfully. She started to move forward, but the Doctor stopped her. Anne saw that her father's face was blank, mask-like, all traces of humanity wiped away. With a shock of horror, she realised what had happened. He had been taken over by the Great Intelligence!

# 11

## 'I want your mind'

'Father,' said Anne again. She took a step towards him. The two Yeti moved menacingly towards her, blocking the way. The Doctor put a hand on her arm.

'No, Anne, don't go near him.'

'It was *you*,' said Jamie accusingly. 'You were the one working with them.'

The Colonel cleared his throat. 'Now see here, Travers, I don't understand what's happening but—'

'Silence!' The word came from Travers's mouth, but not in Travers's voice. The Doctor, Jamie and Victoria had all heard those icy tones before. It was the voice of the Intelligence.

The cold, inhuman voice went on. 'Listen to me. I am the Intelligence. I speak through this man's mouth because it is time for you to understand my purpose.'

The Doctor stepped forward, unafraid. 'What do you want here?'

'You defeated me in Tibet, Doctor. Now you have fallen into my trap.'

'So that's why you brought me here. For revenge.'

'Revenge is a petty, human emotion. My purpose is a greater one.'

'And what is that?'

'I observed your mind during our previous encounter, Doctor. It surpasses that of common humans.'

The Doctor didn't seem particularly pleased by the compliment. 'Get to the point, please,' he said irritably. 'What do you *want?*'

'I want *you*, Doctor—or rather your mind. Its contents will be invaluable to me in my conquest of Earth.'

'And how do you propose to get it?'

'I have prepared a machine. It will drain all knowledge and past experience from your mind. Your brain will become as empty as that of a newborn child.'

'I can resist you, you know,' the Doctor challenged. 'You can't just take me over, like poor Travers. My will is as strong as yours.'

'You must submit to me willingly. Otherwise the machine will not function.'

'And suppose I refuse?'

'Then I shall settle for quantity, rather than quality,' the cold voice mocked. 'I shall drain the minds of all the humans here, and those of many others, until I have the knowledge I need—to complete my conquest. Weaker minds will not survive the shock as yours will. The humans will die.'

The Doctor said calmly, 'If I *do* co-operate, what will you offer in return?'

'The lives and freedom of all your friends.'

Anne nerved herself to speak, 'What about my father?' It was eerie to hear that alien voice from her father's lips.

'He too will go free. I have used him only to communicate my commands.'

'Then he *hasn't* been helping you—before?'

'There are other human hands at my command.'

'Oh yes? Whose?' The Doctor was interested.

The Intelligence seemed to lose patience. 'Do not question me, Doctor. I know that even now you seek ways to destroy me. I must guide your thoughts.'

Travers, or rather his body, took a sudden step forward, grabbed Victoria by the wrist and dragged her back to the door. Jamie and the Doctor leaped to her defence, but it was too late.

The two Yeti stepped forward to form a shield. The Doctor's shoulders slumped. 'No, Jamie. It's no good.'

The icy voice spoke for the last time. 'Co-operate, Doctor, and she will be released unharmed. I give you one hour to decide.'

Dragging Victoria, Travers strode away, the Yeti following him. The door closed behind them.

Jamie made for the door. Lethbridge-Stewart stepped in front of him, barring his way.

Jamie doubled his fists. 'Let me past, Colonel, I'm going after her.'

'Don't be a fool, boy, you can't fight them barehanded. We've got to work out a plan.'

'Work out what you like—I'm going.' Jamie dodged round the Colonel and flung open the door. He found himself facing a Yeti, and hurriedly slammed the door shut.

'I don't think they want us to follow, Jamie,' the Doctor explained gently. 'Not just yet, anyway. Don't worry, Victoria's quite safe. The Intelligence won't harm her if I co-operate.'

Evans, who had been looking on popeyed with astonishment, said, 'Far as I can gather, if this Intelligence thing gets the Doctor here, it'll leave us alone. That right, sir?'

Lethbridge-Stewart nodded. 'That's what it looks like.'

Evans said reasonably, 'Then why don't we just let it have the Doctor, and we can all go home?'

He seemed quite hurt at the storm of reproaches that broke over his head. Anne and Jamie were both talking at once. The Colonel was spluttering, 'Of all the disgraceful, cowardly suggestions...'

Only the Doctor seemed undisturbed. He patted Evans on the back and said solemnly, 'I promise you, if I don't come up with a better answer, I'll hand myself over.'

116

'You will not!' said Jamie hotly.

'You'll have to look after Victoria,' said the Doctor. 'And when it's all over, you'll both have to look after me. If I'm going to have the mind of a baby, someone will have to care for me till I grow up!' He smiled at Jamie's woebegone face. 'Don't worry, I'll try not to let it happen!'

Evans had gone to the door. He was listening intently. 'Ssh!' he said suddenly. He opened the door a crack, then opened it fully. The Yeti had gone. 'Thought I heard it move away,' he said happily.

The Colonel said, 'We'll search the place to make sure. Come on, Jamie. *And* you, Private Evans.'

The three of them went out, leaving the Doctor alone with Anne. 'Come along, my dear,' he said cheerfully. 'We've got work to do. We've got to get that control unit of yours working properly.'

'We've only got an hour!' protested Anne.

'Exactly. So there's no time to waste!' Purposefully the Doctor moved towards the bench, reaching in his pocket for the electronic spare parts he had taken from the shop.

The Colonel supervised the search of the Fortress, reflecting ruefully that his effective fighting force was now reduced to one young Highlander and a very timid private. Pity about Evans, he thought, the Welsh usually made such splendid soldiers.

117

As they came along the corridor Lethbridge-Stewart said, 'Well, no trace of the beast—that last one must have been a rear-guard.'

Jamie was looking thoughtfully at the main door. 'If we tried to follow them through the tunnels we'd mebbe run into it again. But suppose we went up top, got ahead of it, then came down again—we could take them by surprise. And if we could at least find Victoria, it'd give us a better chance to rescue her, when the Doctor does come up with the answer.'

Evans was looking at him in horror. 'I reckon we're a lot safer down here.'

'Aye, *we're* safer,' Jamie burst out angrily. 'But what about Victoria and Travers? Och, if you'll no come with me, I'll go by myself.'

Lethbridge-Stewart sighed. 'Well, at least we'll be doing something. Private Evans, you stay here and guard the civilians.'

'Right, sir,' said Evans, very relieved. He did his best to look fierce and military.

'And don't take any chances,' added the Colonel. 'Come on, Jamie.'

Evans watched them move off. 'Me, take chances?' he muttered. 'You must be joking!'

Jamie and the Colonel came to the head of the stairs and listened. All was silent. 'Right,' said Lethbridge-Stewart. 'Ready, Jamie?'

Jamie nodded. The Colonel flung open the surface door and immediately staggered back. The doorway was filled with a glowing, pulsating mass. The Web had reached the upper level. It started to ooze through the open door and down the stairs.

Jamie leaped forward and helped the Colonel. They heaved desperately on the door but the pressure of the Web was too great. Slowly the door was forced back.

'Secondary fire door, just along the corridor,' gasped the Colonel. 'Go and unhitch it, Jamie. I'll hold on here.'

The heavy metal fire door lay folded back against the wall. It was rusty with disuse and Jamie had a terrific struggle to get it in position. He managed it at last and yelled, 'I've got it! Come on, Colonel!'

Abandoning his struggle with the upper door, Lethbridge-Stewart sprinted down the stairs, the Web rolling slowly after him. He leaped through the half-open fire door, then he and Jamie slammed it shut, securing it with heavy metal bolts. 'The stuff's moving pretty slowly,' gasped the Colonel. 'And even when it gets here this ought to hold it for a while.'

'Aye,' said Jamie drily. 'I hope it does.'

Unaware of the approaching danger, Anne Travers and the Doctor were working busily.

The Doctor had reassembled the sphere and stood looking thoughtfully at it as it lay before him on the bench.

'Now if this thing is functioning, it ought to be picking up the signals of the Intelligence. So why doesn't it move?' The Doctor glared at the sphere which remained obstinately still. 'Move, you stupid thing!' shouted the Doctor, slamming his fist down on the bench in childish rage. Immediately the sphere bleeped faintly, and started to roll along the bench. The Doctor fielded it neatly as it floated off the edge. 'Hah! Success!' he shouted. 'How are you getting on, Anne?'

'Nearly done. Sorry to be so long, but it's a fiddly job.'

'I'll come and give you a hand,' the Doctor promised. But instead he went on playing with the sphere, exactly like a child with a new toy. He put it on the ground and watched delightedly as it rolled towards the door. The door opened suddenly, and the Doctor had to dive for the sphere as it made a sudden dart to escape.

Lethbridge-Stewart looked down at him as he lay stretched out full length, the sphere in his hand, like a cricketer pulling off a spectacular catch. 'What *are* you doing, Doctor?'

Unabashed the Doctor scrambled to his feet. 'I've managed to get the sphere working again.'

'Och, never mind that,' said Jamie. 'We tried to get out by the surface door and...' He told them what had happened.

The Doctor nodded. 'So we can only go the way the Intelligence allows us to go—through the tunnels.'

The Colonel looked at the sphere. The Doctor had put it back on the bench and it was making repeated attempts to roll towards the door, only to be stopped by the Doctor each time.

'Just how is this thing going to help us, Doctor?'

'Well it isn't,' said the Doctor, 'not in itself. But it will help us to test Professor Travers's control unit.'

Jamie was unimpressed. 'Och, is that all? You're not getting on very fast, Doctor.'

Lethbridge-Stewart cleared his throat. 'Must say I agree.'

Anne Travers and the Doctor had been working frantically, and Anne felt that the reanimation of the sphere was a considerable achievement. 'Perhaps we'd get on quicker if you left us alone,' she flared.

Jamie and the Colonel gave each other looks of mutual sympathy, and retreated in dignified silence. As they walked along the corridor, Lethbridge-Stewart said, 'Seems as if it's up to us, Jamie. Since we can't go overground, we'll have to risk the tunnels.' They turned into the Operations Room to find Evans hiding behind the door. He jumped out nervously, covering them with his rifle. The Colonel glared at him. 'What do you think you're playing at, Private Evans?'

'Been working it out, sir. I know *I'm* not working for the Intelligence—so it must be one of you two.'

'Och no, it was yon bloke Chorley,' said Jamie. 'I said so all along.'

Lethbridge-Stewart brushed aside Evans's wavering rifle. 'Put that gun down, Evans, and listen to me. Jamie and I are going into the tunnels. You will remain here. You'd better guard the Doctor in the laboratory.'

'Sooner stay here, sir, if you don't mind. Er—better strategic position, see? I can watch the corridor.'

'Very well, carry on. Come along, Jamie.'


On the platform at Piccadilly Circus a strangely motionless group stood like passengers waiting for a train. In the middle stood Victoria, gripped firmly by Travers. On her other side was the towering form of a Yeti. Travers's hand round her wrist felt like a steel clamp. 'Please Professor, let me go. You're hurting me. I won't run away, not with the Yeti here.'

Travers stared blankly ahead, giving no sign that he'd heard.

A voice boomed out, echoing hollowly. 'Release her, Professor. She will not escape.'

Travers's hand opened, and Victoria pulled her wrist away, rubbing it tenderly. She looked round fearfully.

The voice spoke again. 'There is no reason to fear, child.'

'Who are you? Where are you?'

'I am everywhere,' said the cold, gloating voice. 'I am the Intelligence!'

# 12

## The Fall of the Fortress

There was a strange, crackling sound every time the voice spoke. It amused the Intelligence to make use of the station's public address system. The voice boomed again, and this time Victoria realised it came from a loudspeaker just above her head.

'Travers, you have served my purpose. Awake!'

Travers jerked suddenly and came to life, his old, kindly self once more. He rubbed his eyes and looked round in confusion. 'What's happening, Victoria? Where are we?'

Victoria led him towards a bench. 'You'd better sit down and rest.'

'No, no. Can't do that. Work to do. Got to help the Doctor...' Suddenly he gripped her arm. 'Victoria, don't move. There's a Yeti—'

Victoria sighed. 'I know, Professor, it brought us here.'

Taking her by the hand, Travers began backing slowly away. The Yeti didn't move. They turned to run, and found themselves facing the second Yeti. It growled menacingly. Travers and Victoria moved back to the bench. Hopelessly, they sat down to wait.

The sphere was thudding against the laboratory door, as if trying to make a hole in it. Already the wood was beginning to splinter. 'It'll smash through in a minute,' said Anne.

The Doctor made a last adjustment to the control device. In its final form it was a small black box packed with electronics, controls set into the lid. The Doctor snapped the lid shut, 'Let's see if it works.'

He adjusted the controls. The sphere continued to slam against the door. Anne looked worried, 'Is it on full power?'

The Doctor nodded, readjusting the controls. Still the sphere thudded mindlessly into the door. Anne shook her head. 'It's no good. We've failed.'

The Doctor moved slowly around the room, holding the control box in different positions. He came nearer and nearer the sphere. When he was little more than a yard away, the sphere stopped moving. 'Ah-ha!' he said triumphantly. 'It *does* work—but only at very short range. Better than nothing, though.'

'What next, Doctor?'

The Doctor rubbed his chin. 'We can *stop* a Yeti with this thing—but that isn't enough. We've got to re-programme the sphere to obey our commands. How long have we got?'

Anne looked at her watch. 'About half-an-hour!'

Victoria and Travers were talking in low whispers. 'You're sure Anne is all right?' Travers asked anxiously.

Victoria nodded. 'She's with the Doctor. Don't worry, I'm sure they'll find the answer.' Travers was still very confused and Victoria felt she had to keep his spirits up. Strangely enough this had the effect of making her feel better herself.

There came a bleeping sound, and the nearest Yeti moved away down the platform, disappearing into the tunnel. Travers stared after it puzzled, but Victoria was looking in the other direction. She pulled at the Professor's sleeve. 'Look!' Sergeant Arnold was stumbling along the track; his forehead was gashed, his uniform tattered. He moved nearer. The remaining Yeti seemed oblivious of his presence.

Travers hissed, 'Arnold! Yeti! Hide!' He pointed to the nearby Yeti. A look of understanding came over Arnold's face and he ducked below the platform. Travers and Victoria edged slowly towards him, taking care not to alarm the Yeti. 'Arnold!' muttered Travers again. 'Can you make it back to H.Q.?'

'Think so, sir.' Arnold's voice was faint below them.

'Get back and tell the Doctor where we are.'

'What about you two?'

'We can't move, or the Yeti will attack. But it's guarding us—it doesn't know about you. Off you go, man.'

Arnold crept along the track and disappeared into the tunnel.

Jamie and the Colonel moved cautiously along. Suddenly Jamie stopped. 'Look here!' He picked up a scrap of white linen, edged with lace. 'Victoria's handkerchief. At least we know we're on the right track.'

The Colonel said, 'Listen!' They could hear the sound of footsteps stumbling towards them.

'Doesna' *sound* like a Yeti,' whispered Jamie. It wasn't.

Sergeant Arnold stumbled into view. He saw the Colonel and tried to come to attention, but he reeled and almost fell. Lethbridge-Stewart caught hold of him.

'Sorry about this, sir,' Arnold muttered faintly.

'What happened to you, Sergeant? We'd given you up for dead.'

'Don't really know, sir. I was pushing the trolley into the Web and I blacked out. When I came to, I was wandering around the tunnels. Listen, sir, I've seen Victoria and Professor Travers.'

'Where are they?' asked Jamie excitedly.

Arnold gestured behind him. 'Just back there... Piccadilly. Yeti was guarding them. They said get back to H.Q. ... warn Doctor...'

'And that's exactly what we'll do,' decided Lethbridge-Stewart. 'Come on, Jamie, at least we know where Victoria is now. There's nothing we can do till the Doctor gets his box of tricks working.'

Supporting Arnold between them, they began to move slowly back the way they had come.

Private Evans sat in the empty Operations Room, rifle across his knees. He was uncomfortably aware that he was one of the few remaining survivors among all the soldiers who had manned the Fortress. He was wondering how long it would be before *his* luck ran out. When the little silver sphere rolled through the door and across the floor towards him, he jumped straight on to his chair, like a girl frightened by a mouse. Lifting his rifle he took aim at the sphere.

The Doctor appeared. 'No, don't shoot!' He looked at the sphere and said, 'Stop!' To Evans's astonishment, the sphere obeyed. 'Sorry if it frightened you,' the Doctor apologised.

Evans climbed down from the chair. 'I wasn't *frightened*... Just got up there to take a better aim, see? How did you make it stop?'

'I told it to.'

Evans leaned forward. 'Here, ball, you go back where you came from.'

The sphere didn't move.

The Doctor chuckled and spoke into a small radio-microphone slung round his neck. 'Move back. Stop. Move left. Stop. Now right... Stop.' The sphere obeyed each command. Anne Travers joined the Doctor.

'How about that?' she said proudly.

Evans looked dubious. 'It'd make a smashing toy—but how's it going to help us?'

'Don't you see,' said the Doctor. 'Once we get it inside a Yeti, the creature will obey our commands.'

Evans paled. 'Just how do you get it inside a Yeti?'

'We're going to Warren Street to look for one now. Coming?'

Evans shook his head. 'Me go near one of them things? I may be stupid but I'm not that daft.'

'All right,' said Anne, 'we'll do it on our own, won't we, Doctor?' She held up her hand as the Doctor started to protest. 'It's no use arguing—I'm coming with you.'


Travers and Victoria heard bleeping as the second Yeti returned along the tunnel. It came directly towards them and the other Yeti joined it. Victoria realised they were being shepherded along the platform. 'Where are they taking us?' she whispered nervously.

'I've no idea. Don't worry, we'll be all right.' Travers tried to sound optimistic—but he didn't really believe what he was saying.

*

Now alone in the entire Fortress, Private Evans was more nervous than ever. He tried a quick chorus of 'Men of Harlech', but it did little to lift his spirits. He heard the sound of footsteps in the corridor and peeped cautiously out. To his astonishment he saw Jamie, the Colonel and Sergeant Arnold. 'Where's the Doctor?' snapped Lethbridge-Stewart. 'We looked in the laboratory but he wasn't there.'

Evans was staring transfixed at the Sergeant. 'But... but...'

Arnold, who seemed to be recovering rapidly, growled, 'Don't stand there bleating like a Welsh baa-lamb, Evans, answer the Colonel.'

'The Doctor and Miss Travers have gone back into the tunnels, sir,' said Evans nervously. 'Warren Street, they said.'

'What the blazes for?'

'Said they wanted to catch a Yeti, sir.'

Lethbridge-Stewart shook his head disbelievingly. 'All right, Private Evans. Get the first-aid box over there and put a dressing on the Sergeant's head.'

'Yessir!' Evans ran to the laboratory, fetched the first-aid box and began bandaging Arnold's head with considerably more enthusiasm than skill. Lethbridge-Stewart looked on, wondering what on earth he was going to do next.

Jamie was looking at the indicator map. Suddenly the Warren Street light began to flicker. 'The Web's moving again. We'd better warn the Doctor.'

The Colonel turned to Evans. 'You stay here and finish what you're doing. We'll be back as soon as we can.'

Anne Travers and the Doctor rounded a bend in the tunnel and found their way blocked by a solid wall of the Web. The Doctor sighed. 'No good, we'll have to go back and find another way...'

They turned and suddenly froze—a Yeti was moving down the tunnel towards them. 'We're trapped,' whispered Anne.

The Doctor shook his head. 'Not a bit of it. We wanted a Yeti and now we've found one. Pass me the control box, Anne.'

She stared at him. 'You were carrying it, Doctor!'

'Oh was I?' The Doctor started feeling in his capacious pockets.

The Yeti moved steadily nearer.

The Doctor produced the sphere and passed it to Anne. 'Here, hold this.' He went on searching.

Anne shrank back as the Yeti came closer. It had spotted them now. The red eyes glared menacingly, and it gave a savage howl. Now almost upon them, it raised its paw to strike. The Doctor produced the box from his pocket and touched the controls. The Yeti froze, one arm still upraised. Anne gasped with relief. 'I know it only works at close range, Doctor, but really...'

The Doctor chuckled. 'You weren't worried, were you? Here, take this, and give me the sphere.' He passed Anne the control box, took the sphere from her and opened the flap in the Yeti's chest. Quickly he took out the sphere already there and inserted his own reprogrammed one in its place. He stepped back and spoke into the radio-microphone slung round his neck. 'Now then, you—turn round.' For a moment nothing happened. Then, slowly, the Yeti turned.

Anne gave the Doctor a triumphant hug. 'You've done it!'

'*We've* done it, my dear—with your control unit we should be able to work him over quite a distance.' He looked up at the Yeti and said, 'All right, you can put your arm down.' The Yeti obeyed. The Doctor turned to Anne. 'We must get back to H.Q. Now I know that this works, I can develop a way to block *all* the Intelligence's transmissions.' They set off back down the tunnel, then the Doctor turned. 'Mustn't forget our new friend. Come along, old chap.' Obediently the Yeti lumbered after them.

Evans had finished cleaning the Sergeant's wound, and was now applying a bandage. He tied the last knot and stepped back to admire his work. 'Real professional job that, Sergeant. I should have been a doctor.'

Arnold grunted. 'Well then, Doctor Evans, you can get your medical gear back to the laboratory. Then come back here and start tidying up. This place is a diabolical mess!'

Evans gathered up his things and went out. Trust a sergeant, he was thinking. Fancy worrying about spit-and-polish at a time like this.

Arnold wandered across to the indicator map and gazed blankly at it. So very few lights still burning now... He heard a scream and a clatter and ran from the room.

Evans was standing outside the laboratory, staring into the room with horror on his face. Arnold ran up to him and looked in. The laboratory wall was bulging towards them in a great swelling curve. Even as Arnold watched, cracks appeared, widened. Suddenly the whole wall burst inwards. Through the gap poured the glowing, pulsating mass of the Web.

## 13

## Captives of the Intelligence

The Web poured out of the widening gap, slowly and inexorably engulfing the entire laboratory. Arnold jumped back and slammed the door. 'Come on, Evans—evacuate!'

They tore through the corridors and out through the main entrance. Arnold closed and barred it behind them. 'That'll hold it for a short while. We'd better find the others and tell them H.Q.'s had it.'

Evans backed away. 'Not me, Sarge.'

'Look, there's four people out there. If we don't warn 'em they'll be for the chop.'

Evans didn't move. 'So, four people for the chop then—no reason to make it six, now is there?'

'That's enough lip,' roared Arnold. 'Follow me, Private Evans.'

He marched down the tunnel as Evans turned and ran in the opposite direction. 'Come back, you 'orrible little man,' shouted Arnold. But Evans was already out of sight. Arnold muttered, 'Right, lad, I'll have you for that.' He reeled and staggered for a moment, then regained control of himself. Battered but indomitable, he set off down the tunnel.

The Doctor and Anne marched along, their Yeti following behind like some ungainly pet. Suddenly the Doctor stopped, as he heard footsteps. The Yeti brushed past him, marching on, since no one had ordered it to do anything else. 'Hey, you,' yelled the Doctor indignantly, 'Stop. Turn. Come back. Wait!'

'Why did you stop, Doctor?' asked Anne.

'Someone's coming. Since we still don't know who's working with the Intelligence and who isn't, the fewer people who know this Yeti's on our side the better.'

'How do we keep it secret?'

'Like this,' said the Doctor. He spoke into his microphone. 'Yeti! Remain here for ninety seconds. Then resume acting on instructions from the Intelligence, until you are instructed otherwise. Switch off for ninety seconds—now!'

Leaving the Yeti standing motionless behind them, the Doctor and Anne hurried away down the tunnel. A few minutes later they ran straight into Jamie and Lethbridge-Stewart.

'Och, am I glad to see you,' called Jamie. 'We came to warn you, the Web's moved as far as Warren Street.'

The Doctor patted him on the shoulder. 'It's very kind of you, but we already know. We ran straight into it.'

'Glad you're both still safe,' said the Colonel. 'Any luck with that gadget of yours?'

'Not really,' answered the Doctor evasively. 'We need to get back to H.Q. to run more tests. Any news of Victoria?'

Jamie nodded eagerly. 'She and Travers are being kept prisoners at Piccadilly. Arnold managed to survive the Web—he saw them.'

The Doctor seemed about to speak, but Anne Travers looked at her watch. 'Time's nearly up, Doctor. If we're going to get back to H.Q. and work on the control box...'

The little group hurried back towards Goodge Street. In the tunnel behind them the Doctor's Yeti suddenly came to life. An electronic signal bleeped out, and two more Yeti appeared from further down the tunnel...

As the Doctor and his party were moving along the side-tunnel to the Fortress, they heard footsteps coming towards them. Sergeant Arnold ran up to them. Staggering a little, he came to attention in front of the Colonel and saluted. 'H.Q.'s gone, sir. The Web burst through the wall. Whole place will be swamped by now.'

Lethbridge-Stewart absorbed the news of this fresh disaster with his usual coolness. 'Anyone hurt? Where's Evans?'

'I'm afraid he cracked, sir. Scarpered.'

Jamie heard movement in the tunnel behind them. He swung round. 'Look out—Yeti.' Three Yeti were advancing down the tunnel towards them, their shaggy bulk filling the entire tunnel.

Anne moved closer to the Doctor and whispered, 'Which one is ours?'

'No idea,' he whispered back. 'They all look alike to me!'

The three Yeti moved forward. Behind the Doctor and his friends was only the Web-filled Fortress. They were trapped.

Private Evans was running frantically away from the Fortress when he saw a Yeti coming towards him. He dived into an alcove and crouched motionless. The Yeti lumbered past. With a sigh of relief, Evans jumped out of hiding and ran on, only to encounter a second Yeti. He backed away, babbling idiotically. 'If you're looking for your friend, he went that way!' The Yeti shot out an arm and grabbed Evans by the shoulder. The second Yeti reappeared and grabbed him by the other shoulder. They lifted him clear of the ground, and with Evans dangling between them, set off down the tunnel. Evans smiled weakly. 'Going for a little walk, are we? There's lovely!'

The Yeti herded their prisoners to a junction and then halted. The leading Yeti began sending out signals. Arnold whispered to the Colonel, 'When we move on, I'll try and make a break for it, sir. Maybe these things don't count too well. If I'm on the loose I'll follow and try to help somehow.'

The Colonel nodded. 'All right, Sergeant, it's worth a try.'

The Yeti received another signal, and moved on. As they passed a side tunnel, Lethbridge-Stewart stumbled into the Doctor. In the moment of confusion, Arnold slipped away into the side tunnel. The rest of the party were herded on... Apparently the Yeti had noticed nothing.

Travers and Victoria were taken along the platform, up endless steps, and finally into the ticket hall at Piccadilly Circus. The big round area was silent and empty, and standing incongruously before the ticket office was a large glass pyramid, linked to a throne-like seat. A metal circlet, on a flexible arm, was suspended from the apex of the pyramid, so that it hung above the throne.

Travers moved to look closer at the pyramid. The Yeti warned him off with a menacing growl.

Victoria grabbed his arm. 'Look!' The shadow of a human figure moved in one of the tiled passages leading out of the concourse. 'Who's there?' called Travers. The shadow drew back, and the footsteps moved away.

'Do you think it was the Intelligence?' whispered Victoria.

Travers shrugged. 'I doubt if the Intelligence has a human form. Maybe it was one of its human servants—

like me a while ago.' Travers spoke bitterly, aware how easily he could be brought under control again. 'If only there was something we could do!'

'The Doctor will turn up to help us,' Victoria said confidently. 'He always does.'

'Not this time, my dear. With you as a hostage, he'll have no alternative but to surrender.'

Over the loudspeaker system, the voice of the Intelligence boomed, 'You are right, Professor, the Doctor *must* surrender. He will be here soon. He is our guest of honour. Meanwhile do not attempt to interfere or my Yeti will destroy you...'

The speaker clicked off. Travers groaned. 'And to think that what's happened is all my fault...' He buried his face in his hands.

Down below, the Doctor and his group waited on a platform. It was almost as if they were about to make their entrance in some formal ceremony. Jamie looked at the Yeti guarding them. 'It's a pity you didna' have any success with your gadget, Doctor.'

'Oh, but we did,' whispered the Doctor. 'I'm waiting for the moment to use it.' Swiftly he told Jamie what had happened in the tunnels before they met, and of the Yeti under their control. 'Trouble is I've lost track of him,' he concluded sadly.

'Och, that's a great help.'

'I want you to find him, Jamie. Take this and keep calling our Yeti. He's bound to come eventually.' The

Doctor slipped the radio-microphone round Jamie's neck, hiding it under his wide-collared shirt.

'How will I know if I've got the right one?'

The Doctor grinned. 'You'll soon find out if you haven't. Now then, Jamie, we've got to hide you. I hope you don't suffer from claustrophobia?'

Harold Chorley and Sergeant Arnold ran into each other in a nearby tunnel, to their mutual surprise. Chorley immediately burst into a flood of explanations, telling how he had wandered lost in the tunnels, dodging the Yeti and driven ever back by the advancing Web.

Arnold looked on impassively as Chorley faltered to a stop. 'We'd all forgotten you, Mr Chorley. Wonderful how you managed to survive all that time, isn't it?'

Chorley backed away. 'What are you implying?'

'Just wondering, that's all, sir. And now I think you'd better come with me, don't you?' Arnold gripped Chorley's arm with one of his strong hands, and led him away.

On the platform, the Doctor, Lethbridge-Stewart and Anne Travers were still waiting. Jamie was nowhere in sight.

'Doctor, why not use the control device on these Yeti?' whispered Anne. 'We could get away...'

The Doctor shook his head. 'And leave Victoria, and your father? Besides I'm looking forward to meeting the Intelligence.'

The Colonel looked keenly at him. 'You're going to surrender, Doctor? Arnold's still free—and now there's Jamie. Maybe they'll be able to do something.'

Before the Doctor could reply, two Yeti appeared, carrying Evans between them. They dumped him beside the other captives and moved away. Lethbridge-Stewart glared at him. 'Sergeant Arnold told me you deserted, Private Evans. Didn't do you much good, did it?'

Evans was shocked. 'Me desert, sir? Sergeant Arnold must have misunderstood. I decided to make a heroic attempt to go for help, single-handed you see.' He looked round nervously. 'Er—is Sergeant Arnold here?'

'No... luckily for you.'

Evans looked very relieved.

The Yeti were signalling once more. One of them separated the Doctor from the others. The Colonel made a move to stop them, but the Doctor called, 'No! Whatever you do, don't struggle. Don't try to resist them...' His voice faded as the Yeti urged him away.

Evans shook his head. 'He needn't worry, *I* won't struggle!'

There was a further wait, then one of the Yeti began to herd them after the Doctor. 'Seems as if it's time for us all to get fell in, sir,' said Evans.

The last captives had gone, and the platform was empty. Slowly the lid of a big metal sandbin was raised, and Jamie peeped out from his hiding place.

\*

After climbing endless stairs the Doctor was taken into a tiled passage, leading to the main concourse. A Yeti stood waiting, a strange helmet-like device in its hands. It raised the helmet as if to lower it on to the Doctor's head. 'Just a minute, old chap,' said the Doctor politely— and operated the control device hidden in his pocket. Both Yeti froze. The Doctor smiled contentedly. 'Now then, let's have a look at that contraption.' Reaching up carefully, the Doctor took the device from the Yeti's claw-like hands...

When Anne Travers was led into the main concourse with the Colonel and Evans, she saw her father and Victoria standing motionless before the pyramid. She ran to her father and hugged him. 'Father, what happened? Are you all right again?'

To her relief it was his own voice that answered, the familiar kindly face that looked down at her. 'Don't worry, Anne, they haven't hurt us.'

'What about Jamie and the Doctor?' asked Victoria. 'Where are they?'

Anne put a reassuring arm around her shoulders. 'It's all right, Victoria. They're not far away...'

Feeling, as he said to himself, like some great daftie, Jamie crouched by the end of the platform muttering into the little radio-microphone. 'Come to me. I am at Piccadilly. Come to me.' To his astonishment, he saw a Yeti moving along the track. Jamie was about to step out into sight but decided on a further test. 'Stop! Raise your arm!' The Yeti did neither. It simply lumbered on and out of sight. 'Och, it's no use,' muttered Jamie. 'Wrong Yeti!' He moved towards the platform arch— and walked straight into another one.

The small group before the pyramid looked up as the Doctor came into view, a Yeti close behind him, the strange-looking helmet already in place on his head. Victoria tried to run to him, but Travers held her back. 'Doctor, what are they going to do to you?' she called frantically.

The Doctor seemed quite cheerful. 'Don't worry, Victoria, everything's under control.'

'Indeed it is, Doctor,' boomed the mocking voice from the loudspeakers. 'Under *my* control—as so many humans have been.'

Harold Chorley stumbled into the concourse, a Yeti behind him. 'You,' said Travers angrily. 'You were the one who betrayed us to the Intelligence.'

Chorley was babbling with fear. 'No, it's not me, I wasn't helping the Intelligence. It was him!'

From the entrance behind Chorley a stiff figure walked forward, its face an impassive mask. It was Sergeant Arnold.

# 14

## The Final Duel

Colonel Lethbridge-Stewart listened in shocked disbelief as the icy voice of the Intelligence came from the rugged old soldier who had served him so loyally. 'I chose to use the body of Sergeant Arnold from the first—just as I briefly used Travers. He revealed your plans to me, he concealed my Yeti in your Fortress. Now it is time to begin. This is the start of my conquest. And here is the last member of my party.'

Jamie came forward, a Yeti behind him as guard.

From Arnold's lips the voice of the Intelligence ordered, 'Stand by the Doctor.'

Sullenly Jamie obeyed. The Yeti guarding the Doctor stepped behind him, and a shaggy arm shot out to encircle his throat. Jamie gasped for breath. 'A reminder, Doctor,' said the Intelligence. 'If you resist me, the boy will die. Go to the chair beside the pyramid.'

The Doctor did not move. 'No. I *will* submit—but not until Jamie is released.'

There was a moment's silence. The spectators could almost feel the struggle, as the Intelligence locked wills with the Doctor. Then it spoke again. 'Very well.' The Yeti released Jamie, who staggered back, rubbing his neck. Victoria wanted to go to him, but dared not move.

The Doctor started walking towards the pyramid. Arnold followed. The Doctor seated himself, and Arnold lowered the metal circlet so that it made contact with the helmet on the Doctor's head. 'Soon your mind will be absorbed by the Great Intelligence. Your knowledge will assist my conquest of this planet, and of many more. You should be proud, Doctor.'

'Get on with it,' said the Doctor tersely. 'I just want to get this over and done with.'

'There must be no resistance,' warned the Intelligence. 'If there is, these humans will die. Prepare for a great darkness to cloud your mind.'

Travers, Anne, Victoria, Chorley and Evans watched as Arnold operated controls on the base of the pyramid. The Doctor's face was calm and relaxed as the machine began humming with power. Jamie was too busy to watch. He was slipping the microphone from inside his shirt with agonising slowness and raising it to his lips. 'Attack,' he muttered fiercely. 'Attack the other Yeti now!'

Suddenly the Yeti that had brought Jamie in, the Yeti he had discovered to his delight to be the one re-programmed by the Doctor, lumbered into action. With great sweeping blows it smashed down the two

Yeti guarding the Doctor. 'Now, get Arnold,' shouted Jamie. The Yeti lumbered obediently towards the new target, and clubbed him to the ground. 'Hold back the other two Yeti,' ordered Jamie. As *his* Yeti began attacking its fellows, he ran towards the pyramid.

Arnold was on his feet, seeming unharmed by the blow. 'Yeti, protect the pyramid,' he screamed in the Intelligence's voice.

One of the two remaining Yeti held a Web-gun, which it swung to cover Lethbridge-Stewart. With a sudden burst of courage, Evans knocked the gun from its hand. The Yeti sent him flying with a single blow, and advanced on the Colonel, who dodged quickly away. The Yeti fell back, to defend the pyramid as commanded.

Meanwhile Travers and Jamie had reached the pyramid and, dodging behind the two Yeti, they were trying to drag the Doctor from his seat. To their surprise he resisted furiously. 'No, leave me alone,' he yelled. 'You're spoiling everything!'

Jamie decided the Doctor's will must already be under the Intelligence's control, and increased his efforts to drag him away.

The Yeti were fighting with maniacal fury. By now there were only two on their feet; Jamie's Yeti and one of the two guarding the pyramid. 'Destroy!' shrieked the Intelligence, and the two giants began exchanging great smashing blows.

The Colonel and Evans had joined Travers and Jamie in trying to drag a furiously resisting Doctor from the throne. Their combined efforts heaved him out at last, and all five landed in a struggling heap on the floor. Jamie saw that the helmet was still on the Doctor's head, and still linked to the pyramid. With a desperate lunge he snapped the joining cable, and wrenched the helmet from the Doctor's head. Drawing back his arm, Jamie hurled the heavy metal helmet with all his strength, straight into the glowing heart of the pyramid.

There was a brilliant white flash. A soundless explosion flung them all to the ground. Shakily Jamie picked himself up and looked round. Most of the others seemed unharmed. Victoria was helping Anne sit up. Travers, Chorley, Evans and the Colonel were all struggling to their feet. Jamie noticed with relief that the Yeti were *not* getting up again. They lay sprawled over the ticket hall, smoke pouring from gaping holes in their chests. He guessed that their control spheres had exploded, just as had happened in Tibet. He felt a pang of sorrow for 'his' Yeti, the one which had defended them so bravely. Arnold too lay unmoving.

Jamie looked for the Doctor and found him standing by the pyramid, literally hopping up and down with rage. As Jamie came up to him, the Doctor said furiously, 'Why couldn't you all leave me alone?'

Still unbalanced by shock, decided Jamie. 'Hold on, Doctor, if we hadn't pulled you out, you'd have been a heap of dust by now.' Jamie pointed to the pile of white debris, all that remained of the pyramid.

'I told you to leave me alone,' the Doctor repeated crossly. 'Now you've ruined everything.'

Colonel Lethbridge-Stewart, Professor Travers, Anne and Victoria had joined them. Jamie glared angrily at the ungrateful Doctor. 'What's all the fuss about, we've won haven't we?'

'No, we haven't,' shouted the Doctor. 'Not a complete victory.'

Lethbridge-Stewart gestured round at the shattered pyramid and the still smoking Yeti. 'Looks pretty complete to me.'

Seeing the happy faces all round him, the Doctor shook his head and smiled, his bad temper forgotten. 'Forgive me, all of you. You weren't to know. You see it was such a splendid little scheme. I'd managed to switch off my Yeti guard and reverse the polarity on that helmet thing before they brought me in. The Intelligence wouldn't have drained my brain—I'd have drained the Intelligence! Instead we just got a giant short-circuit!'

'Then where's the Intelligence now?' asked Anne. 'Did we destroy it?'

'I doubt it. It's back floating around in space somewhere. All we did was to snap its link with Earth.

Look!' The Doctor turned over Arnold's body which was lying face down. The features had crumpled into a horrifying death-mask. The Doctor sighed. 'Poor fellow.'

The Colonel stood beside him, looking down at the body. 'I just don't understand. Sergeant Arnold was so brave, so loyal. He took such risks to help us.'

'When the Intelligence wasn't in control, Arnold was his normal self,' explained the Doctor. 'Unfortunately the Intelligence could take over his mind and guide his actions whenever it wanted. Afterwards, Arnold had no recollection of what he'd been doing. I suspected it was him when I heard he'd come through the Web unharmed.'

Harold Chorley came over to the Doctor. Now the danger was past, he was fast recovering his old brag and bounce. In fact, he was almost back to his objectionable self. 'Well done, Doctor,' he said fulsomely. 'A splendid achievement.'

'Not really,' said the Doctor. 'I'm afraid I failed.'

'Nonsense, Doctor. You're a hero. I'm going to make you world famous! First thing is for you to give a Press Conference...'

The Doctor backed away. 'Why don't you discuss it with the Colonel? He's very good at organising things.'

Chorley said, 'Good idea,' and went off to buttonhole Lethbridge-Stewart.

The Doctor turned to Jamie and Victoria. 'Come on, you two, I think it's time to leave.' They slipped out through a side exit and made their way down to the Piccadilly Line.

The little group in the concourse went on chattering excitedly. 'I reckon the least I deserve is a promotion,' Evans was telling Anne optimistically. 'I could end up a colonel myself.'

Colonel Lethbridge-Stewart was lecturing Professor Travers. 'What the world needs is a permanent International Organisation to deal with this sort of thing. A kind of Intelligence Task Force... I think I'll send the Government a memorandum...'

Harold Chorley bustled up. 'Now then, Colonel, I was just telling the Doctor...' He looked across the hall. 'I say he's gone. They've all gone.'

Professor Travers said, 'He's off to his TARDIS, I imagine. He disappeared rather mysteriously last time we met.'

Chorley snorted. He couldn't understand anyone wanting to *avoid* publicity. 'Now about this Doctor chappie—I never did get the *full* story. Professor Travers, you met the Doctor first, in Tibet, I believe. Can you tell me all about him?'

Travers shook his head. 'I only know a very little about the Doctor, Mr Chorley, and I don't think you'd believe me if I told you...'

The Doctor and his friends had passed through Leicester Square, and were now approaching the spot where they'd left the TARDIS. Under their feet they crunched a crystalline powder, all that remained of the Web. 'The mist will have gone too, up top,' said the Doctor. 'They'll soon have things back to normal.' As the TARDIS came in sight the Doctor suddenly stopped. 'In fact I'd better get us out of here right away,' he said dramatically. 'We might soon be in the most terrible danger!'

Victoria felt she couldn't take any more excitement. 'Oh no, Doctor, what's the matter now?'

'Well, as soon as they can they'll get the Underground running again. Just think we might get run over by a Tube train! And after all we've been through, that would be most undignified!' The Doctor hurried up to the TARDIS and opened the door. Jamie and Victoria looked after him.

'He's mad,' said Jamie indignantly. 'Mad, I tell you. No telling where he'll land us up next.'

Victoria smiled. 'Come on, Jamie, time to go!'

They followed the Doctor into the TARDIS. The door closed and after a moment a strange wheezing, groaning sound filled the tunnel. Slowly the TARDIS faded away. The Doctor and his two companions were ready to begin their next adventure.

# About the Authors

Terrance Dicks

Born in East Ham in London in 1935, Terrance Dicks worked in the advertising industry after leaving university before moving into television as a writer. He worked together with Malcolm Hulke on scripts for *The Avengers* as well as other series before becoming Assistant, and later full Script Editor of *Doctor Who* from 1968.

Working closely with friend and series Producer Barry Letts, Dicks worked on the entirety of the Third Doctor's era of the programme starring Jon Pertwee, and returned as a writer – scripting Tom Baker's first story as the Fourth Doctor: *Robot*. He left *Doctor Who* to work first as script editor and then as producer on the BBC's prestigious *Classic Serials*, and to pursue his writing career on screen and in print. His later script writing credits on *Doctor Who* included the 20th anniversary story *The Five Doctors* broadcast in 1983.

Terrance Dicks novelised many of the original *Doctor Who* stories for Target books, and discovered a liking and talent for prose fiction. He has written extensively for children, creating such memorable series and characters as T.R. Bear and The Baker Street Irregulars, as well as continuing to write original *Doctor Who* novels for BBC Books.

### Mervyn Haisman and Henry Lincoln

Mervyn Haisman and Henry Lincoln worked together on scripts for various TV series in the 1960s, including *Doctor Finlay's Casebook*, *Emergency Ward 10*, and *Doctor Who*. They also wrote the script for the 1968 horror film, *Curse of the Crimson Altar*.

Two of their *Doctor Who* scripts featured the Yeti – robot servants of an alien intelligence – which proved very popular and memorable. The second of these stories, *The Web of Fear*, also introduced the character of Colonel Lethbridge-Stewart who – promoted to Brigadier – became a regular character when the Third Doctor worked with UNIT during the early 1970s. Their third script together, *The Dominators*, was credited to the pseudonymous Norman Ashby and featured the robotic Quarks.

Haisman, who had previously been an actor, and managed a theatre company, continued to write television during the 1970s and 1980s. He died in 2010, aged 82.

Lincoln, who had also been an actor under his real name of Henry Soskin, developed a fascination with the mysteries surrounding the French village of Rennes-le-Chateau and scripted and presented a series of documentaries about it for the BBC in the 1970s. He co-authored the book *The Holy Blood and the Holy Grail*, much of which was based on his own research and ideas. Many of these were incorporated into Dan Brown's phenomenally successful novel *The Da Vinci Code*. Lincoln now lives and works in Rennes-le-Chateau.